D0056793

Drawing the Ocean

Also by Carolyn MacCullough

Stealing Henry

Falling Through Darkness

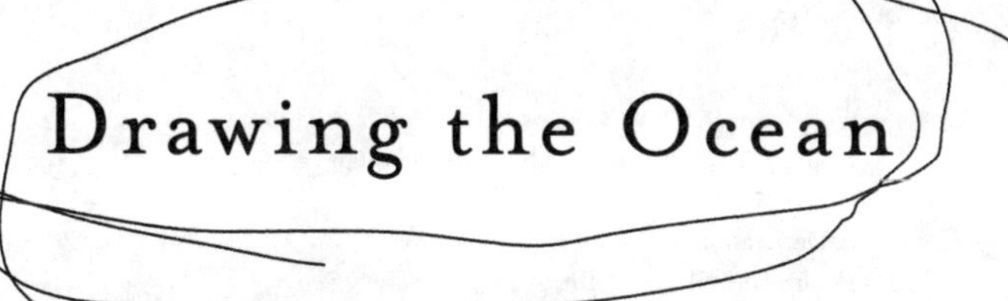

Drawing the Ocean

CAROLYN MACCULLOUGH

A Deborah Brodie Book
ROARING BROOK PRESS
NEW MILFORD, CONNECTICUT

A Deborah Brodie Book
Published by Roaring Brook Press
Roaring Brook Press is a division of Holtzbrinck Publishing Holdings Limited Partnership
143 West Street, New Milford, Connecticut 06776

Distributed in Canada by H. B. Fenn and Company, Ltd.

Library of Congress Cataloging-in-Publication Data

MacCullough, Carolyn.
Drawing the ocean / Carolyn MacCullough. – 1st ed.
p. cm.
"A Deborah Brodie Book."
Summary: A gifted artist, Sadie is determined to fit in at her new school,
but her deceased twin brother, Ollie, keeps appearing to her.
ISBN-13: 978-1-59643-092-1
ISBN-10: 1-59643-092-3
[1. Twins–Fiction. 2. Brothers and sisters–Fiction. 3. Death–Fiction. 4. Ghosts–Fiction.] I. Title.

PZ7.M1389Dra 2006
[Fic]–dc22
2005031471

10 9 8 7 6 5 4 3 2 1

Roaring Brook Press books are available for special promotions and premiums.
For details, contact: Director of Special Markets, Holtzbrinck Publishers.

Book design by Patti Ratchford
Printed in the United States of America
First edition October 2006

Acknowledgments

Thank you to Denise and Gloria Johnson for talking to me about their memories of Tunisia, although Tunisia barely made it into this book! Thank you, as always, to my family, but especially to my sisters—Lisa MacCullough, for reading this book at the critical stages, and Jennifer MacCullough, for all her willingness to brainstorm with me. Thank you to Theresa Benaquist for reading these pages aloud so I could hear the words. Thank you to both Deborah Brodie and Simon Boughton at Roaring Brook Press for publishing this book. And last, but never least, thank you to Frankie Adamo (a.k.a. FFQ) for always saying the right thing at the right time.

Chapter One

The sky on this side of the country looks different, less gauzy, and I wonder if I can get it down on canvas or if it will elude me the way the copper-blue of the California skies did for so long. I'm not ready to try for color yet, so I leaf through my sketchbook until I come to a blank page. I take a breath, run my fingers down the smooth white space before making the first charcoal marks. Quick glances to the sea and the way the gray Atlantic waves curl and hiss across hard-packed sand, as if this is a test and the answers are all right before me. I draw for a long time, long enough for my brother to finally appear beside me.

"Do you like it here?" he asks, after attempting a handstand at the edge of my pink towel.

My fingers keep moving as I think about this question. I like the new house, especially my room in the cupola, the way the walls are round and resist all the square angles of my furniture. I have never lived in anything quite like it. And I like being so close to the beach, close enough that when I can't sleep at night, I pretend that the whole house is a ship that might slip its anchor at any moment and sail slowly, majestically off on the moonlit sea. Better than thinking about how I am starting a new school in a week and how many things could go wrong. Or not wrong, but not exactly right, either.

I had spent long dreaming hours on how to fit in at my new school. How it would be a chance to start over and not be that weird girl anymore who was seen talking to herself sometimes and who was *way* too into art. I had to make friends early and fast. And act normal. I was positive I could do it. But stepping off the plane and on the drive to the new house, I was suddenly not so sure.

And of course Ollie reads my mind and says, "There you go. There's your first friend now."

I squint into the distance, where I know he is pointing at a tall boy dressed in jeans and a bright orange T-shirt. At first I think he is sitting on a folded-up chair, but then I realize it is a closed briefcase. He is scribbling into a white rectangle of a notebook and I wonder if he is drawing, like me. He looks about my age. "Him?"

"Why not? Go talk to him."

"Ollie. I'm not you. I can't just talk to anyone." I study this boy again.

"Come on. Go tell him a story."

"Oh, what do you know anyway? You're twelve." I watch as the boy sets aside his notebook, stares out at the water. "He does look kind of lonely," I concede, turning back to my brother.

Who is no longer sitting by my side.

I put up one hand, shield my eyes from the suddenly too-bright sun, watch a woman walk past me, burdened by a wide striped umbrella. Three small boys dragging towels almost the exact shade of the sea follow in her wake.

"I hate it when you do that," I say softly to the empty space beside me.

The woman cranes her neck, throws me a startled look, then glances back at her children. I return to my sketchbook, exchange my charcoal for my fine-point pencil. I don't say another word.

My brother, Ollie, died four years ago, and I've learned from experience that people don't handle it so well when I start talking to him.

Chapter Two

"Go over there," my mother urges. She shapes each word slowly as she does when she wants to convince me how important something is.

"Where?" my father asks, coming up to us, a glass of red wine in each hand. He offers one to my mother.

"Those two girls," my mother whispers, accepting the glass. "I think Sadie should introduce herself." My father looks over at the food table, nods, winks at me.

"Nice party," he says noncommittally.

A corner of my mother's mouth trembles downward. She takes a sip of her wine.

"Okay," I sigh. "I'll go." I wander over to the table, peel away a paper plate from the stack. Our new neighbor, Marie, has just placed a platter of hamburgers and hotdogs in the center of the table, and I watch the pinky-brown juice drip and ooze onto the white china. I am standing directly behind the two girls now, and quickly, I try to study their clothes to decide if I look all that different.

They are each wearing artfully frayed jean shorts, shorter than my mother would ever let me cut my own, the kind you buy, anyway, rather than make yourself. I note the high-heeled wedges, laced around tiny ankles, the straps crossing in a complicated pattern.

Then the girl directly in front of me flicks back her hair so that it whips me in the face. She glances over her shoulder.

"Sorry," she says, her voice careless.

"It's okay," I answer, and I wonder if this counts as conversation. I watch as they each load up their plates with lettuce and slices of tomato and pickles, bypassing the meat. Then they come to a stop at the center of the table.

"What is this?" the girl asks, staring at my mother's brass bowl, her upper lip curling delicately away from her teeth.

"It's *mechouia*." I edge closer, pick up a triangle from the basket of toasted pita bread my mother also brought.

She divides a look between me and her friend. "Moo-*what*?"

"It's a Tunisian delicacy. My mom is kind of on this kick–studying food from all around the world and–" I make a dipping motion toward the dish. "It's a lot of roasted red peppers and garlic and um . . . olive oil."

"Fattening," she pronounces.

I shrug. "It's good." But even I can hear how unconvincing I sound. I had helped make it, whacking heads of garlic into submission, peeling the hot peppers to reveal their soft, slimy undersides, and now I wish my mother could have made something safe, like potato salad.

"I'm not taking any," the other girl says decisively to her friend, and they both walk away to a corner of the room. Three younger boys fall in behind me, picking up hamburger patties with their bare hands, slapping two hotdogs apiece on their paper plates, jostling me until I step away from the table.

I don't look at my parents. I don't want to check in with my mother's worried-hopeful face. Instead, I slide open French doors and walk out onto a deck dotted with brightly flaming buckets of citronella candles. Below me, the ocean crashes against the rocks.

I pass a man and a woman who are smoking and drinking and apparently having a hilarious conversation, because the woman keeps giving a high shriek of a laugh and slapping at the man's arm. "No, Harry," she is saying over and over. "That is just too much to handle." I think it's Marie, and then she turns, still swatting at Harry's arm, catches sight of me, and I see that it *is* Marie.

"Hi, honey!" she enthuses, and pulls me into her side. She crushes my face against her chest for a minute, and I inhale baby-powder deodorant and the sweetish thick smell of alcohol. "Having a fun time? And where are your lovely parents?"

"They're inside," I answer in my best talking-to-adults voice.

"Sadie and her parents just moved from California. L.A."

"Livingston. A little farther north than L.A." I try to free myself by inches.

"That's right, that's right," says Marie encouragingly, and Harry nods at me.

"L.A., hmm? See any movie stars?" Harry booms at me, and I jump a little, sure that he was not talking this loudly to Marie.

"Um . . . " They are both peering at me intently. "I'm not really good at that kind of thing." They nod as if I have said something wise.

"No, of course not. That's right, honey," Marie agrees. She drains the rest of her glass, holds it out to Harry. "Would you?" She trills a laugh.

"Your wish is my command," he says. "Sadie, anything?"

"No, thank you," I answer hastily. He turns, walks away, steps through the open French doors.

"He's a catch," Marie muses, tightens her arm around my shoulders. She leans against the railing and I do, too. "When you get to be my age, Sadie, there aren't many of them like that. My mother always said that and I never believed her, but . . ." Marie shakes the pointer finger of her free hand up at the stars. "She was right, the old bat!"

"Really?" I ask, not sure where I should come into this.

"I was young and foolish and I was determined to concentrate on my career. I didn't have time for any of that love and marriage and babies stuff."

"Oh." I think for a minute. "What's your career?"

She peers at me. "A little of this, a little of that." Then she releases me, turns. "But you don't want to hear an old woman ramble. There are some very cute young gentlemen in there."

I shrug.

"Or," she says, lowering her voice and leaning toward me, "do you have a boyfriend back in California? Pining away for you under the orange trees?"

I can't help it. I laugh. Then I instantly feel bad. "No," I say truthfully, and there is an apologetic note in my voice. "I don't. No one's pining."

"Hmm." She seems disappointed. "Well, never mind! You'll take them by storm here. Ah, thank you, darling," Marie purrs, turning and holding out her hand for the glass Harry is handing her. Ice cubes clatter faintly.

"Well," I say. "I should find my parents." I step away from their entwining forms.

"Go find those young men instead," Marie replies with her sudden shrieking laugh. She and Harry turn back to each other.

But I don't go find the young men. I take one last look through the doors and see my parents locked in conversation with a woman wearing a rainbow-striped dress and a wide silver belt. I slip down the steps and follow the narrow, winding path. The walk is strewn with rocks, and more than once I stumble, but I keep my hands out for balance, and finally bump up against the low seawall. Shells and pebbles embedded in the hairy sea moss prick at my palms as I scramble up and over. A pause to free my feet from sandals, then I am trekking across sand as cool as powder. I take a deep breath, drinking in the salty tang of sea air, and try to imagine the color it might be, swirling into my lungs. Black-violet, maybe.

A bonfire is burning about a hundred yards to my right; dark figures criss and cross around the flames. After a minute, I swing left and begin following the seawall. I pass our house. It looks tall and awkward in the moonlight, as if when stretching up on its toes to look out over the ocean, it unbalanced a little. I keep walking, counting the houses I pass, some of them painted with bright squares of windows, some of them still and dark. I stop in front of one, figuring that the people aren't home and so they won't mind that I'm sitting almost in their front yard. I stare out at the ocean and think about Ollie and how he might have liked it here for real. It's getting harder to tell with him.

Flecks of light dance and glitter on the surface of the restless water. When I was younger, I truly believed that those chips of light came from the lamps of the houses of the sea people. As deep as I dived, I never found the start of the spiraling magical path made of snail shells and crushed glass that would lead me to the doors of the kingdom. Ollie said he believed that too, but I don't know that he really did.

The August night air feels heavy and wet, and my jeans are too warm. But they are my favorite pair–I crocheted flowers onto the knees after seeing the idea in a magazine. I was particularly proud of them until I saw what those two girls tonight were wearing. I pick at a piece of colored yarn now and wonder if I should stuff these in the back of my closet for weekends only.

I roll them up, wade into the ocean, the water colder than I expected. I stand motionless, letting the tide foam around my shins, enjoying the feel of sand sliding away beneath my heels. The moon is a perfect hole of light punched through dark sky.

There is a rough scraping sort of noise. I jerk my head

sideways to find that someone is sitting on the wall. From the profile angled a little away from me, I can tell it's a guy, and for one irrational second, I am convinced it's Ollie.

"Hey," I whisper. If it *is* Ollie, he isn't acting in his normal way, looking over and grinning at me from somewhere. Ollie never liked to be by himself when he was alive; he was always hanging around. Sometimes it drove me a little crazy. Then I bite down on that thought. If I could have Ollie back again, I would never, never, never mind if he were always around.

Now I hear the unmistakable sound of someone unzipping a bag. After a rustling few seconds, a small disc of light springs into existence. Whoever is holding the flashlight rifles through the bag some more, and then a second unmistakable sound–flicking pages. The light steadies in one spot.

I smile to myself, in solidarity with this unknown reader. Then I begin to think about who would actually come out of a house onto a deserted beach at night to read. *You could ask him*, is what I imagine Ollie would say. I think about whether I can do this. I can't stand the idea that whoever this is will look at me the way those two girls looked at me tonight and decide I'm not worth it. I chew my lip for a minute, and despite the cool water rushing past my ankles, despite the vast night sky and blank, blank sea, I suddenly feel hot and crowded with worry.

Then I decide this person can't be all bad, especially if I thought he was Ollie, so I splash forward three steps until I'm standing on wet sand. The light bobs and flickers in an alarmed way.

"Hey, over there!" I call out, and wait.

The light hones in on me, travels up and down. I wait some more.

"Hello." A guy's voice comes out of the darkness. The light freezes to my face and I shield my eyes.

"Hi," I say again, now feeling stupid standing here, sandals hanging limply from one hand.

Silence.

"Um . . . could you get the light out of my face?"

"Sorry," the voice comes again, and the light obligingly bounces off to the side.

I walk forward a few paces. "How come you're reading on the beach?"

"I like it here at night." The words are quick and bitingly crisp.

"Yeah, but to *read*?"

"I like reading."

I think about this for a little while. "Okay," I add.

"*Okay?* That's it?"

"Well . . ." I shift. "Um . . . "

"And we started out so well. You were sassy, telling me to get that damn light off your face, I was—"

"I didn't say *damn* light. I just said *light*." I don't know what's happening to me, but somehow in the dark, I can be braver. "Okay, what's your name?"

"Boring," he pronounces instantly. "What's in a name?"

"What are you reading?" I try.

A pause in which I count two waves breaking. "Better. T. S. Eliot's poems. Ever tried them?" And now his voice is a mocking challenge.

I search, I scramble, I dig. The rapture on my tenth-grade teacher's face. Ms. Phelps comes briefly back to me. *"I have heard the mermaids singing, each to each. I do not think that they will sing to me."*

"I'm grudgingly impressed." But he doesn't sound grudging, he sounds delighted. The light flips back to him, illuminating his face in trembling waves. I can't get a definite impression of his features, except to decide that they are interesting enough in their angles to make me want to draw him. And even though he is smiling at me, I think his eyes are the saddest eyes I have ever seen. Almost as if he reads my mind, the light snaps back over me.

"And here I thought I wasn't going to meet a mermaid ever. Wonders never cease and all."

"I . . . aren't mermaids usually in the water?" I ask, wondering if I am really having this conversation.

"You were."

"I have legs."

"Details."

I laugh a little, waiting for him to join me. When he doesn't, I say, "I'm new here. My name is–" The light skids suddenly, brightly into my eyes, and I put up one hand, step back. It feels like a slap.

"Don't ruin the mystery. Once we know each other's names, it's all over with."

"What do you mean?" I say, feeling more than slightly irritated.

"Oh, you'll see. Let's just keep this memory to ourselves, and when we're old and gray, then we can take it out and treasure it."

"I think you're–"

But a car horn is blaring, breaking across the insistent thrum of waves.

There is a quick, scrambling noise, the whine of a zipper. "Well, must run. Whoever lives here must have just come home," he says.

"But don't you live–"

"It's been lovely. I'll always remember you."

"Hey–" I try again. Bewildering and sort of annoying as he is, this has been the first real conversation I've had with anyone my age since I moved here. Not counting Ollie. And how much can you count him anyway?

But the light clicks off and I hear footsteps squashing the sand as he retreats. I watch his long, lean form leap up the slope, round the side of the house, and then only blank air, empty canvas is left.

I begin to pick my way back along the wall, counting the houses again until I reach my own.

The living room lights are already on and each darkened downstairs window suddenly snaps into the picture as my mother tears through the rooms with frantic energy. I sigh, feeling a familiar prickle along the back of my neck.

"Well, you could have told them you were leaving," Ollie says from somewhere next to me.

"Shut up," I say to my brother.

Chapter Three

Just as I am wondering if I could stand in the doorway of the school's main office unnoticed all day, someone sweeps by me. I flatten into the frame of the door as a girl with dark, impossibly straight hair that hangs almost to her waist, curves into the room. The scent of her perfume fills the air immediately. She sinks into one of the chairs outside the tightly closed oak door that bears a plaque reading, MR. ANDERSON. She looks at her fingernails, frowns, then transfers this frown directly to me.

"What?"

Instantly, I pin my gaze directly over her head, as if riveted by the framed glossy photographs of school assemblies. A phone rings endlessly, insistently.

"You're new here."

I risk looking at her again to find that she is examining me thoroughly. I nod.

"Lucky you," she mutters. I stare at the glittery silver heart on her sky blue T-shirt, aware that this is the second person my age I've talked to all summer, and I can't think of anything brilliant to offer. I wonder if she knows the boy with the saddest eyes in the world. Somehow, I feel this is not the time to ask.

"Are you the one who got dropped off in that car?" she asks.

My mother had driven me to school this morning. She had gotten flustered at the school entrance and nosed the car into the bus-only lane. As if this were a signal, all the docked buses began blowing their horns, and an irate traffic guard in a mustard yellow vest pumped her arm in the air three times. My mother gripped the wheel and muttered something under her breath that I knew I wasn't meant to hear, and swerved until we were back in the right lane. I ducked my head, made my escape from the car, and didn't look up until I was safely inside. Now, I nod.

"My mom," I say.

"What's the matter? Driver's day off?"

I hate her instantly, and this must show on my face, because her eyes, ringed with silver glitter that matches the heart on her T-shirt, widen before she smiles.

Mr. Anderson's door swings open, revealing a glimpse of leather chairs and a brass lamp perched on the edge of a desk. A short, round woman wearing a purple dress and an astonishing number of rings and bracelets bustles out and closes the door behind her with a decisive click. She looks up, catches sight of me, and beams.

"Sadie?"

"Yes, ma'am."

From behind the woman's back, there is a faint snicker, but if the woman hears it, she gives no sign. "Sadie Caldwell, right? I have your schedule here. And welcome to Pioneer Mountain High. Although we really have no mountains here. No mountains at all." She makes a little harrumphing noise, still beaming, and I realize this is supposed to be funny. I nod quickly, not daring to look at the girl with the long black hair.

"Anyway, I'm Mrs. Clemont and, if you have any questions, any questions at all, you *must not* hesitate to come to me, dear. That's what I'm here for." She bobs her head at me a few times before circling over to her desk. I watch as she ruffles through some papers and then, seemingly at random, pulls a blue folder free from a stack of blue folders. She flicks open the cover, scans the contents. "Okay. Your first class is Chemistry Is Everywhere. Now isn't that delightful?" She smiles at me and I blink.

"Yes, but I–"

"Now let's see. First period bell doesn't ring for ten minutes, which means we have time for a tour." She closes the folder, taps it against the edge of her desk, bunches her mouth into a tight bud. Then she suddenly appears to notice the other girl for the first time. "Ah, Lila," she says, the warmth in her voice soaring outward to reach all corners of the office. "This is Sadie, our new student from California. Since you're obviously free, you can show her around." Mrs. Clemont checks her watch, smiling pointedly. I think if Lila were a dog, she would be growling now.

"I'm not free," Lila says in the bored voice that I am beginning to think is permanent. "I actually need to see Mr. Anderson."

"Well," Mrs. Clemont begins, spreading her hands wide, her rings and charm bracelets catching the fluorescent light. She hooks her thumb over her shoulder with an exaggerated motion toward the closed and silent door, lowers her voice. "He's busy right now. Why don't you come back during lunch?" She draws out the word *lunch* for what seems like a long time before her lips flex back into a pleasant smile.

"Fine." Lila sighs, and gets to her feet languidly, as if thinking of something else. She pauses just outside the office door, turns her head to reveal a perfect-looking profile. "Are you coming, Sophie?"

"Go along, dear." Mrs. Clemont encourages me with a shooing motion, as if I were a baby bird she needs to shove out of the nest. The phone begins to ring again.

I swing my backpack up and over my shoulder, trudge after Lila. "It's *Sadie*," I murmur to the back of her neck. At first I think she doesn't hear me, so I say louder, "It's Sadie!" What is it with the people around here and names?

"Whatever," she calls back.

After a minute, I fall in at her side, trying to slow myself down to match her ambling pace down the hallway.

"Let me see your schedule," she says, holding out one hand without looking at me. Her nails are brilliantly polished semicircles. I surrender the blue folder that Mrs. Clemont gave me.

Lila glances at it for a minute before pronouncing her verdict. "Boring. You've got Snooze and Snore."

"Snooze and Snore?"

"Yeah. Mr. Snore for English, and Ms. Snooze for World History. They're having an affair." Then she turns to me and widens her eyes dramatically, puts a finger to her lips. "Top secret, of course."

"Really?"

She snorts. "No way. Everyone knows. It's pretty pathetic."

"Why?"

"He's married." She flips back her hair, says almost dreamily, "He hit on me last year. When we were working on the school play."

"What happened?"

"What do you think happened?" She looks sideways at me as if daring me to come up with a hypothesis. "Anyway, art's your elective?"

"Yeah. Painting. What's yours?"

"Acting."

"That makes sense," I find myself saying, and then swallow quickly. But she doesn't seem to notice.

"Yeah. It's, like, the only thing I want to do. I can't wait to graduate. My mom wants me to go to Princeton because she didn't get to go. But, whatever. As soon as I finish here, I'm off to New York City."

I try to take all this in, but we are passing through a set of heavy glass doors and then we are suddenly standing in a large room full of what seems like hundreds of students. The air smells of old food and Pine-Sol, and I try not to breathe in deeply.

"Student center," Lila says, resuming her bored voice, as if suddenly remembering her tour-guide duties.

"It's so huge," I breathe.

"Yeah. It's an acre, actually. We have lunch here and our free periods here, too." She looks back at my schedule. "Nice. You have lunch at eleven ten. Love that."

I can imagine my mother's voice in my head, nudging me forward. *When do* you *have lunch?* "Um . . . when do you–"

"Science wing over there. Arts and Gym back down the hallway. Your English and World Studies classes are going to be over there." She points directly ahead of us to yet another set of glass doors. "And your Math class will be there, too, actually. Library's that way. Watch out for Mrs. Block. She's the worst." She pivots and faces me. "Okay, tour over." She flaps my folder at me, and I catch the edge of it. I clutch it to my chest.

"Thanks, Lila."

"No problem, Sadie," she says, and flashes me a sudden, almost-real smile. "You'll be okay."

She strolls toward a large table full of students. Two girls look up, squeal out her name, and rush to hug her. I look away, let my gaze go unfocused so that everything blends and blurs into a softness. I swallow down hard against a particularly bad missing-Ollie moment.

The bell rings and I turn and head in the direction of the Science wing.

❧

At 11:11, I skirt the periphery of the student center, looking for an empty table. But the only one is smack in the middle of the

huge room and I can't bring myself to walk to it. The folds of the brown paper bag that hold my lunch are slippery in my sweating fingers.

My eyes are drawn to the library, but I have a feeling that the Mrs. Block Lila warned me about won't allow any eating in there, and I am surprised to find that I am hungry after all. This leaves the great outdoors, so, without looking at anyone, I inch along the border of the room, weaving my way around clumps and knots of people, heeding the inner siren call of the red EXIT sign.

I push hard at the door; it opens just enough to allow me to squeeze through, and then I am free in the sunshine. I cross away from the parking lot, avoiding the Phys Ed field, where a soccer game is in progress, and round the bluffs where a few kids are hunched in small circles, furtively sucking on cigarettes. I concentrate on the dimming of all noise and head toward a small grove of trees.

It is only when I look up that I realize how far from the school I have walked and that I am not alone after all. There is a flicker of movement as someone steps out from behind a tree and I hurry forward eagerly.

"Oll–" My brother's name crumbles in my throat. Not Ollie.

"Well, well, so she goes to school after all. And here I thought mermaids never left the ocean."

I blink at him, take in the picture by daylight. He is tall and thin, with thick brown hair that stands up in spikes. His cheekbones are high, and he wears narrow, black-framed glasses and a bright yellow T-shirt that says in jagged blue letters, CEO OF NOTHING.

"Details," I say finally, wishing I had been a little quicker.

But he smiles just the same, pushes his glasses farther up the bridge of his nose, and asks, "Feeling out of place yet?" Then he winks, turns, walks completely into the woods.

I consider for a minute, decide to follow. The air smells clean and fresh, shimmering in the heat. I stop by a large-limbed tree, put my hand out to touch one thick-veined leaf, loving the way the light filters through it to create a hundred different shifting shades of green.

And that is when the whistle jars me out of my reverie.

"Excuse me!" a sharp voice is calling behind me, and I whirl to face a tiny woman in a pink sweater set. She is urgently waving at me from the edge of the blacktop. "Come out of there, please," she says, and the *please* is so preemptory, nothing to do with the actual meaning of the word, that I feel a sudden burn of anger, even as I comply.

"I'm sorry," I begin, but she is shaking her head. She steps forward and I stare down at the blades of grass brushing across her ankles.

"No students allowed in the woods."

"Oh, I didn't know."

"School rules," she states. Her eyebrows pinch together tightly as she pulls her high heels free of the grass. "Back inside at once." She seems to be waiting for me to walk ahead of her, so I stumble forward.

"I'm sorry. I'm new here," I murmur, cradling my lunch bag in my arms. "I just wanted to eat outside."

"That's all right," she says, her voice softening by one degree. "But in the courtyard only, in full view. No going into the woods. Ever."

"But what about–" I begin, then bite down on the words. She doesn't seem to have heard me anyway. She steps back onto the concrete with a satisfied click of her heels and holds open the door as if not trusting me to come back inside on my own. I turn and cast one last look at the woods.

Just as I thought. Empty.

Chapter Four

The last of the buses depart the traffic circle, leaving behind a few stragglers, lone islands in the sea of concrete. None of them are the boy from the beach, now the boy from the woods. As I wait for my mother to pick me up, I try to arrange my face for her.

"It's not that bad, Sadie," my brother's voice says. I look sideways, my eyes tracing over the outlines of Ollie's legs. As usual, they are in motion.

"Easy for you. You're dead. You don't have to go to school," I mutter to my drawn-up knees.

There is a silence, a kind of glaringly loud silence. "Sorry," I say, and look up to find two girls standing several feet away from me. One of them is looking in my direction, and she leans over and whispers to her friend, who then also turns and pinpoints me. Great. Here one day only and already I am making a name for myself. My plan for being normal is going just swimmingly.

I look sideways again. My brother sticks out his tongue at me, crosses his eyes, disappears. I put my hand on the bench where he was sitting next to me, tighten my fingers around the wooden slats, try not to cry.

A horn blows, light, tentative, a tap of a sound. My mother is waving through the open passenger-side window. As I walk to the car, I hear a burst of giggles from behind me.

We file into the house, and my mother, who had been so carefully quiet as she drove us home, now becomes animated. "Wait until you see," she says as she rushes past me. I hear a rustling in the kitchen, and then a bright, tinkling sound, and my mother reappears in the foyer. "Look what I found," she cries. "The wind chimes." She holds aloft the hollow ceramic pipes and charms strung through with delicate wire that I made in eighth-grade art class. "Where should we put them?"

"Over a doorway?" That's where they hung in the house in California. I had read somewhere that it was supposed to be for good luck. I move past her into the kitchen, crunch through some Styrofoam bits, and head to the refrigerator.

"Wait," my mother calls behind me. "I made cookies and lemonade." She points to the mahogany breakfast table that has been wedged into one corner of the room.

"So?" my mother begins, pouring lemonade into a wineglass. I take it, count three pits in the murky liquid, swallow carefully. My tongue cleaves to the roof of my mouth, trying to escape the tart puckering exploding across my taste buds.

"Mmmmm," I say, reaching for a cookie. My best guess is peanut butter.

"So, how was it?" My mother asks again. I notice that she is not drinking her own lemonade.

"It was good," I say, chewing. Not peanut butter. Maybe salt cookies. I put the rest of the cookie down next to my lemonade, wishing for a glass of water.

"And what about the other students? Did you meet any nice girls?"

"Yes. I met a very nice girl named Lila and a boy." Here I stumble because I don't even know his name. "Um . . . he seemed very nice, too. And the Student Center is an acre big, and everyone sits there for lunch and free periods."

I chatter on and on, encouraged that my mother is absorbing each and every word, her hands folded neatly in her lap, like a child listening to a favorite bedtime story. Finally I run out of bright words, and my mother leans back as if exhausted.

"I'm so happy it went well," she says, picks up her lemonade, takes a swallow. "Oh!" She makes a face. "Nice and sour, right?"

"A little." I unfold my legs, stand up, stretch. "Well, I've got some homework."

"Already?" my mother cries.

"Can you believe it? I have to write an essay about the most important person in my life so far."

"Really?" She arches her neck a little and I laugh.

"You're on the list." I pivot, step carefully around three boxes. "Oh, Mom, I think I need to start taking the bus."

"But is that safe?" From where she is sitting, she reaches up to the windowsill, repositions a bowl filled with round polished rocks. "I read about a bus crash in this community only three years ago." Her voice wavers, drops. "Four children were injured. Thank God, nothing serious, but–"

"Everyone else takes the bus." I pause. "Actually, a lot of them drive. And speaking of which, I think they're handing out the Driver's Ed forms this week, to start soon."

My mother picks up a handful of the rocks, lets them fall through her fingers, back into the bowl, with tiny, precise clicks.

"I don't want you to drive yet."

I turn back slowly. "Mom. I'm past sixteen. Most people have their license at this point. At least let me apply for my learner's permit. The school," I say, my words coming out a little bit ragged now. "They have classes . . . on Tuesdays. We learn driver-safety rules. Then you or Dad could–"

"I don't think so, Sadie. Not yet." Her voice has firmed and evened. I will have to appeal to higher authorities.

"Is Dad home for dinner tonight?"

She gives me a look. I know enough to leave the kitchen at that point.

Chapter Five

"Bug," my father calls as the front door slams. "You home? Bug?"

I set down my brush, wipe paint-smeared fingers on my smock, listen to my father's footsteps evenly measuring the stairs. When we were younger, my father used to call Ollie and me Clatterbug and Chatterbug. The first time he called me Chatterbug after Ollie died, something in my mother's face closed, and my father looked as helpless as I had ever seen him. But a few months later, he started calling me Bug, and it stuck.

"Up here," I call from the attic, where I have staked out my studio. My father comes through the doorway, looking excited, his hands circling through the air loosely.

"Anything good?" I ask. He and my mother have been up since dawn, antiquing. My mother is always bringing home what she calls "gems" of furniture, poring over their lines and searching for their pedigrees in one of her antique furniture manuals. She makes detailed plans to strip and refinish each piece. When we moved from California, the collection we left behind could have furnished two houses at least.

"Come see," my father says, folding my hand, paint stains and all, into his. He leads me downstairs, past my mother, who is flapping a tape measure at a heavy chest of drawers she must have just bought.

"Parker, this would fit perfectly in the living room," she calls as we pass by.

"Yes!" my father shouts back, pulling me outside to confront a shiny ten-speed Schwinn the color of a neon banana. "Look," he says proudly. "Look at that, will you? A real bargain. Only been ridden once, and the owners were getting rid of it for practically nothing." He beams at me. "Now you have some transportation, right?"

I stare at him. He releases me, goes over to the bike, and strokes the chrome handlebars lovingly, taps the gear shifts. "What do you think? It even has a bell, see?" He presses a little lever jutting out of a round knob on the right handlebar. A tiny merry chime pings.

"Did you talk to Mom at all about letting me sign up for Driver's Ed?"

My father's fingers work the gear shifts faster.

"Dad?"

"I did, honey." He doesn't look at me. "She thinks maybe it would be better if you waited just a little."

"Waited? How long?"

He shrugs.

"How *long*?"

"Until you're eighteen."

"That's ridiculous!" I explode. "*Why?* Why don't you trust me?"

"Sadie," my father says in his somber voice that means I am supposed to pay attention to whatever it is he is about to impart. "We do trust you. It's the–"

"Yeah, yeah. The people around me. People hit bike riders, too, you know."

My father drops his hand away from the gears as if burned. He stares down at the bike, and then without another word, turns, goes back inside.

The grass beneath my feet swims and blurs into a sea of green. The bell on the bike dings once, twice, and I look up at

Ollie, who is impossibly balanced on the long narrow seat, grinning at me. "Maybe you could even get a basket," he muses.

"You're so lucky I can't throw anything at you."

"Come on," he says. "You would have thought this was a pretty cool ride at one point."

"Yeah, when I was *twelve*, Ollie," I say, swiping at my eyes.

Chapter Six

"Wakey, wakey, rise and shine! Good morning, good morning, good morning, everyone!" Mr. Hutchinson says as he sweeps into the class. I bite my lip. On the first day, I was the only one who had answered his cheery (and identical) greeting, prompting three girls to turn around and stare at me before falling across each other in peals of laughter. So I keep my head down.

"*Wokay*, everyone," Mr. Hutchinson says, holding up his hands. "*Whoa-kay*."

Lila, who is whispering steadily to some other girl, looks at me briefly, rolls her eyes toward the front of the room. I try to roll my eyes back, but she has already turned away.

"Whoa-kay," Mr. Hutchinson says for the third time, snapping the classroom lights off and on repeatedly.

When we are slightly quieter, he says, "Open your books to page forty-seven. Judging from everyone's dismal efforts on Monday's take-home, we're not understanding the basic building blocks of trigonometry." He nods importantly at us. "I'm glad this happened though. You know why?"

"Um, you want us to fail?" someone ventures.

"No, Mr. Novak," Mr. Hutchinson chides gently. "No, indeed. But if you were all perfect this early in the semester, I'd have nothing to teach you, right? *Right?*"

I glance around, note that a few people are nodding, so I risk a quick bob of my head, only to find Lila eying me.

"So," Mr. Hutchinson says, and claps his hands together loudly. "Page forty-seven."

I open my book to the appropriate page, prop it upright, and pull my sketchbook out of my bag. Mr. Hutchinson's voice buzzes, narrows, fades out as I swirl and swoop my pencil, shadowing my page with the limbs of the Hanging Tree. My fingers pause near the top of my drawing, and then slowly, as if through no will of my own, wings and feathers unfurl from the tip of my pencil.

❧

The day Ollie and I turned ten, we decided to conquer the Hanging Tree. No one knew exactly why it was called that, but everyone had been forbidden to climb it. The sky was the color of salt, and leaves skittered and whispered in the faint breeze. I could tell Ollie was scared by the way he approached the tree, like he was walking underwater.

"I'm doing it," he said at last, his back to me, and I came forward, knelt, cupped my hands. His foot sprang into my palm, then away, and before I could rise, he was scrambling up the tree. "Come on," he called down to me, so I stretched and swung myself up.

I climbed steadily, swiftly, overtaking my brother as we both angled for the same strong middle limb. I flung my arms out and, by virtue of being one inch taller than Ollie, I managed to get ahead of him. Then I paused, trying to smooth back my breathing.

"Sadie," Ollie whispered, his mouth barely framing the words. "Look up."

I lifted my chin, millimeter by millimeter, until my face was pointed toward the sky. The largest crow I had ever seen was perched directly above me, so close that I could see the ragged tips of coal-colored feathers. Its head swiveled, its eye beaded into mine, and I stared deep into yellow-black depths.

I opened my mouth, never knowing what I might have said, because just then, the crow called once, a fierce short burst of sound as it took flight. Black wings beat just inches from my face, and I clapped my hands up and over my head. There was a *whoosh*, a crashing, a snapping of branches, and then I was flying.

I felt my brother kick his legs frantically, his hand just brushing my shoulder, his fingers closing convulsively on my shirt before there was the sound of tearing cloth. I spiraled down in free fall. Black wings exploded before my eyes as I hit unforgiving earth.

I screamed. Or tried to, but my lungs felt like limp sails, unfurling uselessly inside my body. I tried again. This time I managed to produce a sort of coughing moan, and then my vision cleared.

Ollie's worried face was the first thing I saw. He brushed careful fingers across my cheeks, held up two ragged night-black feathers.

"These were over your eyes," he whispered. "That's why you couldn't see. Can you . . . are you . . ." Then he glanced over his shoulder, looked back at me, the outer shell of his green irises suddenly eclipsed by dark pupils.

"It was all my idea, Ollie. Only mine," I had time to whisper. Then my parents, my mother a half stride ahead of my father, swept past Ollie, ignoring him. I felt my mother's hands on my shoulders, the only thing anchoring me, because suddenly I felt like I was falling all over again, although I knew the earth was solid underneath my back.

"Sadie," my mother said urgently, as if summoning me, and as her face began to blur and fade, I realized that I had never seen anything so beautiful and terrible as the look in her eyes.

❧

"You're pretty good," a voice intrudes, and I jump a little. Mr. Hutchinson has his back to the class and is covering the blackboard with formulas, the chalk squeaking every so often between his fingers. Most of the other students are whispering to each other. I look at Lila, who has turned my sketchbook toward her and is assessing it.

"Is that supposed to be you?" she asks, her long index finger circling Ollie's half- hidden form in the tree.

I shrug. "No. Yeah, I guess. It's just a drawing."

She leans back, looks at me. "Do you want to be an artist?"

"When I grow up?" I say, trying for a little sarcasm, but her face remains impassive. "Yeah, maybe."

She seems about to say something more, but Mr. Hutchinson whirls abruptly, points toward the ceiling with his piece of chalk. "Pop quiz time, folks," he announces in his jarringly cheerful voice. I look at the clock, realize that half the class has passed and I haven't even turned one page of my book.

There is a collective groan, then a slamming and shuffling of books. Without turning, the boy sitting in front of me thrusts his arm out, waves a sheaf of white papers. I take the stack, keep one for myself, pass the rest back.

I examine my page, begin to balance the integers, positive for negative, until they equal zero, making sure to detail each step. Beside me, Lila gives a gusty sigh, kicks one strappy sandal against the chair in front of her until the girl she was talking to looks back with a stealthy air, shrugs.

Lila taps her hand against the side of her desk, slowly extends four fingers. I hesitate, look toward the front of the room. The top of Mr. Hutchinson's head gleams pink under the fluorescent lights. I slide my paper to the very edge of my desk and wait. The sky outside the window is an achingly bright blue, and I watch as three black dots wheel and then fall out of sight.

"One more minute, people," Mr. Hutchinson bells out. Lila leans back. I pass my paper forward as the bell rings. "End of chapter three review for homework."

I stumble to my feet, begin zipping up my backpack. It is my lunch period, and I move as slowly as possible, anything to delay the moment when I will have to walk into the Student Center, find an empty corner of a table, and sit for twenty-two minutes, trying to eat the dry-as-paste tuna-fish sandwich my mother insisted on making for me this morning.

"Sadie," Mr. Hutchinson calls as I step away from my desk. I freeze. "May I speak with you for a moment?"

Lila shakes her hair out of the knot on her neck, all expression on her face smoothed away as she walks out the door. Slowly, I move up to the front of the room. I can't bring myself to look at my teacher. Instead, I study his folded hands on the desk, noting the way reddish gold hair curls over each knuckle.

"Listen, Sadie," he says. "I know you're new here, and I just wanted to let you know that if you're having any trouble in the class, you can come talk to me anytime. If ever I'm going too fast, I just want you to say, 'Hey! I need some help here.'" He waves his arms over his head, his face stretching into a parody of distress and concern.

"Okay." I step back a little. "Thanks, Mr. Hutchinson."

He winks. "Call me Mr. H. All the kids do."

Chapter Seven ❧

I stop in the girls' bathroom, splash water on my face, then spend a long time patting it dry. The stalls are all empty. I have only my reflection for company as I apply and reapply three layers of the Strawberry Sweet lip gloss that my mother bought me as a "going to school present." Then I spend at least two minutes repositioning the tortoiseshell barrette in my hair.

"Come on, you have to tell me," a girl shrieks, bursting through the doorway. She is followed by another girl, and they both catch sight of me at the same time.

I retreat to a stall, locking it behind me, wait out their whispered conversation by reading through all the messages scrawled on the gray walls of the cubicle: *China loves Billy, Debbie Gives Good Head,* and *Have a nice day.* Below this in tiny letters someone else has written, *What if we are all part of someone else's dream and that person decides to wake up?*

Finally, the outer door creaks, closing out the bright block of noise. The *plink, plink* of the faucet dripping is all that's left. I unlock the stall door, step out. Ollie is leaning against one of the sinks.

I work the soap dispenser. Watery pink liquid squirts into my cupped palms. My voice is very low as I say, "I can't do it, Ollie."

"It'll get easier."

"What if it doesn't?"

"Well, it's not going to get any easier if you're hiding out here in the bathroom."

I scrub the slick soap off my skin, keep washing my hands long past clean, until the bathroom door slams open again and four more girls stomp through. They crowd around the sinks and begin fluffing out their hair. I edge my way to the door, Ollie side-shadowing me.

"Come on," he says. "I'll walk you in there."

"Thanks." The slightest of words, my lips barely moving as we make our way down the mostly empty hall lined by closed classroom doors and into the overly lit, echoing Student Center. I sigh, scan the room.

"How about there?" Ollie says. The boy from the woods is sitting all alone. An open briefcase rests on the table and every inch of the laminated wooden surface is covered with papers. I can't decide if he spread them out to keep other students away or to keep himself company. All around him, people carrying full lunch trays or brown paper bags pause, their heads turning and turning, their gazes barely registering him.

"It's like he's not there," I say softly. No wonder Ollie likes him so much. I take one step, then another, then another, toward him.

"Sadie," someone says in a low voice, and fingers pinch at my wrist. Lavender shampoo. Lila. I half turn. "Walk with me." She weaves her way through the tables expertly, her hips never seeming to touch the closely packed chairs, and since our hands are still locked together, I can only stumble in her wake. Finally, we step free, and she looks back at me, her cool gray eyes assessing. Then she shakes her head at me. "Are you trying to commit social suicide?"

"What do you mean?"

"Sitting with Fryin' Ryan is the surest way to get yourself branded as a Lifetime Loser in this place. Okay? Jesus, it's like I have to tell you everything."

I am about to ask Lila what exactly else she has told me, but another question pushes its way forward. "Who?"

"Fryin' Ryan. Loser." She gives a delicate shrug, spins on one heel toward a table full of girls. "God, where have you been?" she calls out, saunters forward to embrace a girl with a multitude of long, snake-thin blond braids. "I *love* your hair."

"Really? They did it for me in Barbados," the other girl answers, shakes out her hair, the tiny beads on the end of each braid sliding across each other with faint *click*s.

"Lucky," Lila says, tugging lightly on three braids at once. "How was the place?"

She holds up a tiny pink phone. "No reception. It was supposed to be this high-class resort, and I couldn't get a signal. The place sucked." Her glance flickers over me, stops.

I inch backward slowly, carefully, then concentrate on the long wall in front of me. Someone has spray-painted in bold red letters,

IF YOU CAN BEAR TO HEAR THE TRUTH YOU'VE SPOKEN
TWISTED BY KNAVES TO MAKE A TRAP FOR FOOLS.

Two custodians in blaringly green uniforms, armed with buckets and sponges stained pink, are scrubbing away at the edges of the letters. I transfer my gaze to the oversized digital wall clock, which tells me that there are fifteen more minutes before I can escape to World Studies. I wonder if my classroom might be empty right now. The image of a clean blank blackboard and rows of unused seats washes through my head, tinted in soft sepia tones. I try to pivot like Lila just did, with a sense of purpose.

"Sadie," Lila calls again. "Sadie, this is Erica. Erica, Sadie. Sadie's from California."

Mascara-coated lashes sweep up and down; then Erica looks

at Lila for a second before offering me a polite smile. "Hi." Then to Lila, "Have you seen Travis yet?"

Lila looks up at the ceiling. "Are you ever going to get over him?"

Erica shrugs. "Who says I'm not already?" From the way she flips open her phone, I can tell she is lying.

"Come on," Lila says suddenly, and leads me over to the table, where two other girls are sitting. "Ruth, Christie, this is Sadie. Be nice to her."

The two girls glance up at me briefly, smile as one.

"I like your jeans," Ruth, I think, says after an appraising minute.

I look down at the daisy patches on my knees. "Thanks." I search for a similar compliment, but Ruth and Christie have gone back to talking to each other.

"Morons," Lila murmurs to me. Then she adds in a more considering whisper, "But nice." She pulls out a chair. "Sit." She pushes me backward.

I land in the chair, straighten myself out, wait until Lila sits next to me. "Is this because I helped you on the quiz?"

She arches an eyebrow at me. "For a smart girl, you ask stupid questions." She rests her chin on folded arms. After a minute, she says softly, "Thanks."

Nodding, I lean back, set down my lunch bag. A quick look over my shoulder reveals that the table where Fryin' Ryan was sitting is now full of a group of Asian students.

"So why is Fryin' Ryan called Fryin' Ryan?" I ask. Even though I am talking to Lila, the other girls swivel my way.

"He's so annoying," Ruth begins.

"He's in my Civics class this year," Christie groans. "He's already asking his stupid questions."

"But–" I say.

"Because," Lila answers patiently, "in seventh grade, Ryan told everyone that he was adopted and that his real father was a murderer. About to be electrocuted. He described the whole process, how the veins in your eyes crack and pop–"

"Gross." Ruth moans. She puts down the bunch of grapes she has been eating.

"Some people got upset and, anyway, our principal called home and found it wasn't true. His parents had to come into school for a conference and everything."

"He's sooooo weird," Erica says. She is studying me. "I saw you the other day, outside, talking to him." Now Ruth and Christie are staring at me. I look at Lila, but she has tipped back her chair and is gazing at the ceiling. "Do you *know* him or something?" Erica persists.

I shake my head. "No," I say, and wait, Erica's eyes like two searchlights sweeping across my face. Finally, she shrugs, stares at her phone again as if waiting for it to ring.

I can breathe again. Hearing a faint rustle, I turn back to find Lila poking through my lunch bag. "What's this?" she asks, peeling the waxed paper off my sandwich. "Tuna! I love tuna."

"Be my guest," I murmur.

❧

My mother and I file into the house together. This time, the kitchen table holds a big bowl of cut-up fruit. Even my mother can't wreck fruit.

"Well," she beams. "And how was today?" She closes her thumb and forefinger on my chin as if to hold my face still. Her breath makes warm puffs on my skin. "What's this?"

"Oh," I say, shrugging. "We were bored during Open period, so Lila was putting some eyeliner on me." I had been skimming down the hall, intending to head for the library, when Lila appeared at my side.

"I just got my new theater makeup kit and I need to practice on someone." I had spent most of the next period washing my face.

"So you and this Lila are becoming friends?"

I squirm away from my mother's questioning gaze. "Maybe."

"Well . . . you could invite her over."

I shrug. "It's too early," I say to my shoes, picturing the look of disappointment that is probably crawling across my mother's face right now. "Maybe next week?" I look up and my mother nods vigorously.

"Next week. Just let me know. There's a coconut cake recipe I want to try anyway."

"Um . . . I think she might be allergic to coconut."

Chapter Eight

On Friday, when I enter the art room, the spicy-sharp scent of turpentine pricks at me and I inhale happily.

"Welcome, welcome," a large woman in a blue caftan calls as she billows over to me. "You're my new one this year, aren't you?"

I nod, eyes fixated on the turquoise and tigereye chunks of her necklace.

"Well, I'm Mrs. Byrd. Big Byrd, some of the kids like to call me, don't think I don't know it." She leans closer, and the cracked webs around her eyes deepen and spread. "Come over here. We're doing a still life today in oils. Since you're early, take your pick of easels." She waves one hand toward the forest of waiting easels, moves off to the front of the room.

"Thanks," I say. "Could I have a–" A flutter of pink comes flying by my head, and I reach out one hand, snatch the smock, stiff with paint stains, out of midair.

I check the slant of early-morning light drifting in through the floor-to-ceiling windows, narrow in on the corner of the room where the sunshine spreads in lemony pools. But the easel I want is already occupied. By Fryin' Ryan. He is sitting on a stool, his briefcase at his feet. He glances up from his paperback book, gives me a lazy smile.

"Welcome to my office, mermaid." He is wearing suit pants and a purple T-shirt with a picture of Elvis eating a banana. The word HUH? is spelled out in fat black letters right above Elvis's head.

"You know," I begin casually, and then finish in a rush before he can stop me, "I have a name, and it's Sadie!"

"I like it," Ryan says after a minute. Then he leans closer, whispers, "But I know it's not your real name. Mermaids *never* give their real names to mere mortals."

Even though I remember Lila's warning, I can't stop my smile. I glance toward the front of the room, at Mrs. Byrd as she zips around the still-life composition, her hands darting in and out, rearranging flowers in a brick red vase. I slip the smock over my head, tighten the strings.

"I didn't know you took art," I say after a minute.

"I don't."

"Then what are you–"

"Now, Ryan," Mrs. Byrd says from behind me. "Sadie is here for art."

"Aren't we all?" His gaze is limpid behind his glasses.

"Yes," she says with some asperity, "but *you* are here on my good graces, and *she* wants that easel. It has the best light."

"I know," Ryan replies thoughtfully. "That's why I chose it." He makes a tipping motion with his book.

"It's okay," I say quickly. "I can choose another one."

"No. Ryan," Mrs. Byrd says, and her voice is measured, as if she will start counting at any minute. "We have an agreement here."

"Really," I say, backing up as far as I can. But Mrs. Byrd is a human wall, and I can move only so far. "I'll–"

Ryan hops down off the stool, picks up his briefcase. "No harm done. I wouldn't want to get in the way of an artist and her masterpiece." He salutes both me and Mrs. Byrd, threads his way through the easels to the farthest, darkest corner of the room. "I'll just sequester myself back here. Hold my calls, please, would you?"

"Thank you, Ryan," Mrs. Byrd calls. She puts her arm around my shoulders and presses me toward the stool he has just vacated.

The first bell rings, and it seems to go on and on. Under its echoing clamor, Mrs. Byrd says, "Ryan comes into my class during his free periods. He's a bit . . . troubled." She speaks out of the side of her mouth, elaborately, carefully, and the back of my neck burns.

I am sure he can hear her.

❧

"Why does everyone hate Fryin' Ryan?" I ask Lila at lunch as she pokes through the contents of my brown paper bag. Apparently, Tuesday's tuna fish wasn't sufficiently alarming. I watch her examine my peanut-butter-and-apple sandwich, take an experimental nibble, and then discard it in favor of the Twix bar that I had squirreled away in my bag. She tears the wrapper with her teeth, snaps off the end of one chocolate stick.

"Because he's *weird*," Erica answers from across the table. "Weird beyond weird." She snaps her gum, frowns into the distance as if this is a problem already solved. Then she opens up her backpack. "I brought in some popcorn," she says to Lila. "Want that?"

Lila tilts her head, considers the bag Erica is holding out to her, takes it with her free hand. "Mmmm. Salt *and* sugar. Two of my favorite food groups."

Chapter Nine ☙

"Sadie," my mother calls, but I don't answer right away. It was a game we played when I was little, and she would hunt for me through our house in Livingston.

Maybe because I took up less space, it felt like there were a thousand more hiding spots. Whole unused rooms full of my father's collections of furniture, tall copper samovars, earth-colored wooden masks with empty eye sockets, all the things he collected on his journeys.

It will be only a matter of minutes until she finds me in the attic studio. I glance at the walls, lined with drawings of the ocean, before turning back to my easel. I paint as fast as I can. Gray, green, a hillside and a headstone, and far below it, the blue of the sea creeping over golden sand.

I wasn't allowed to go to Ollie's funeral. Every night for a week after he died, I wandered the house like a lost and angry ghost, bashing into suddenly unfamiliar corners and tripping down flights of stairs that I was sure had never been there before. Sometimes I would find myself outside my parents' door, listening to the muffled sounds of my mother and father crying.

Finally, I would drag my blanket down into the courtyard where Ollie and I had sometimes slept. I would lie on my back under the white netting of stars, until each pinprick of light dimmed.

"There you are, Sadie," my mother says. It is too late to shield the painting from her. "Oh!" One hand twitches upward. "Why do you insist on painting such grim subjects?"

I shrug. "It's for art class," I say, even though it is not. "We have to paint a still life." I mix some gray into the green on my palette, trying to add the tiniest edge of shadow along the headstone.

My mother gives a little huff of a laugh. "We have a bowl of fruit. Or flowers."

"A still life can mean many things," I say in my most superior voice. "Sometimes the Dutch used to paint a still life to indicate mortality. They used to include symbols of death to remind us that the clock was always ticking."

She pauses for a minute, her shoulders stiff. She hates even the near mention of Ollie.

"You were looking for me," I remind her.

"Your father and I have to go to a dinner at the club on Saturday night. It's one of those things where they honor the board of trustees." She gives a shrug, as if to say, *You know I don't want to go, but your father is helpless on these occasions without me.* "I'm sure I can get Marie to come and stay with you. Maybe you can rent movies and make popcorn–"

"Mom," I start, and then stop, watching the flinch travel across her face. Rolling the smooth wooden brush handle between my fingertips, I try again. "Mom," I say more gently.

"I know you're not a child, but I thought–"

"Actually, Lila asked me to come to a friend's house with her."

"Oh," my mother says, and the sun spreads across her face. "What other friend?"

"Erica," I murmur. Erica herself hadn't asked me. Just announced at the lunch table that her parents were out of the house on Saturday and did we all want to come over? Lila had nodded as the bell rang. I had wadded up my brown paper bag and was heading toward the trash can when Lila asked what time she was picking me up.

"Lila," my mother says now, invoking the name, and I nod. The corners of her mouth curve up.

"Yeah. She said she would drive me."

And just like that, the lines of my mother's face sag down. "Oh, honey, I think that . . ."

I smash and grind the bristles of my brush through gray paint until I can hear all my past art teachers give a collective shout in my head.

"Your father and I can drive you–"

"Mom!" I say, cutting ruthlessly across her words. "I am trying to fit in here, and it's not easy when I have to rely on you and Dad for rides everywhere and you won't even let me get my learner's permit and . . . " My voice cracks. We stare at each other. "Lila is seventeen. She's had her license for six months already. I will call you when I get there," I say to her retreating back.

The door slams shut behind her.

I fling a dripping arc of paint across the canvas.

❧

"I'm bored," Erica announces, her voice floating up from her lounge chair.

I am the only one swimming in Erica's pool. Ruth and Christie are arranged on lawn chairs while Lila is dry on her perch of pink flamingo float. She dips her fingers in the water, creating a tiny current, sending the float skirling away across the glistening blue surface. The reflection of the white-as-paint clouds shimmers with the motion.

I tread water rhythmically, watching pool light spiral down my arms and legs. The pink flamingo bobs closer.

"You look like the Lady of Shalott," I say to Lila.

"Who?"

"You know. From Tennyson's poem. The one we were reading two days ago in English. *Lying, robed in snowy white/That loosely flew to left and right/The leaves upon her falling light/Thro' the noises of the night/She floated down to Camelot.*" I give the float a little shove. "Were you paying attention at all?"

"No," she yawns. "That's why I have you." Then she slides her sunglasses down the bridge of her nose, fixes me with a mock severe look. "Caldwell," she says, because she has now taken to calling me by my last name. "You're an odd one." But she grins, and somehow *odd* doesn't feel so wrong when she says it like that.

"I'm bored," Erica moans again.

"Yeah, we're all getting that impression," Lila answers, her voice dry. "So what do you want to do?"

"Call Travis Hartshorn?" Erica suggests with a giggle.

"And hang up again? Aren't you getting a little sick of that game?"

Although Lila's voice is evenly weighted, I sense the slightest lick of scorn. Christie and Ruth exchange glances. I lift one hand out of the water. Tiny silver bubbles bead and cling to my skin.

"So, what are you suggesting?" Erica's voice reminds me of a breeze that sweeps in right before a storm.

Lila shrugs. "Why don't you actually talk to him?"

"What would I say?"

"Tell him to come over." And now Lila's voice is patient and coaxing, a mother to a child.

"Then he'd know–"

"That you like him? He knows anyway. Everyone knows. It's obvious. What does it matter if he *knows*?"

Erica is staring at her, mouth open. "What's with you, anyway?" Her gaze shifts to me. "What are *you* looking at?"

A shadow passes under my churning feet. Ollie, wriggling through the water.

"Not much," I find myself answering.

Over by the lounge chairs, I hear Christie give a little gasp. Then Lila calls out lazily, "Hey, Caldwell, give me a push to the steps, okay?"

I swim over, tread water with my legs, and grasping the pink flamingo by the neck, I pull it to the shallow end of the pool, holding it steady for Lila until she alights on the steps. She climbs out of the water, picks up her flame-colored sarong, and whips it expertly around her hips.

"Well, ladies, it's been a blast." She walks the length of the pool in narrow, delicate steps, stops, looks down at me. "Coming?" Her gray eyes hold just the slightest hint of a challenge, but there is no question for me.

"Sure."

❧

We fly down the highway, the wind pouring through Lila's powder blue Beetle until it seems like my hair will be torn from my head. I am cold, but I make no move to roll up my window.

"Here, take the wheel for a second." Lila twists in her seat, unfastens her bikini top. I look at my hands, but they won't move from where they are resting in my lap.

"Sadie!"

My left hand shoots out and I correct the swerve of the car. Lila takes the wheel back, and I subside into my seat. "You might want to work on those reflexes," she advises, but there doesn't seem to be much reproof in her tone. With her right hand, she steers; with her left, she loops her bikini top over the driver's-side mirror. I watch red tropical flowers flare in the streaming wind.

"Your turn," she says, her skin gleamingly bare in the half light. "And then let's go drive by some teachers' houses."

"Why?"

"Why not," she answers calmly enough. "You can tell your grandchildren about it."

I consider this reason. After a minute, I reach up one half-hearted hand to undo thc clasp on my bikini top. And so when the blue-and-red lights flash briefly behind us, I think my first reaction is relief. Followed by a heart-lurching skip forward to my mother and father's terrified faces.

Lila slows, pulls to the side of the road, and I feel the car shuddering beneath us as if it wanted to race to the finish.

"What are we–"

"Be cool," Lila says quick and fast, scrambling into her tank top. But I notice the faintest quiver in her voice.

I nod, stare straight ahead, trying not to look at the dark shadow that comes to a looming stop against the driver's side.

"Evening, girls," a deep voice says. I study the way the shimmering lines of Lila's headlights cut through the dusk. A flashlight travels through the car, skips away, like an overgrown lightning bug.

"Evening, officer," Lila says, and her voice has suddenly turned Southern. I want to ask her who she thinks she is playing, but this doesn't seem to be the right moment.

"Have you girls been drinking?"

"No," Lila says.

There is a small silence, and I can't help it, I turn, stare at the cop. He seems overly tall next to Lila's little car. Tall and wide, like a wall. A solid, angry wall. "No, sir," I echo, and his gaze shifts back to Lila.

"How fast do you think you were going?"

"Um . . ." She taps her chin with one finger as if this is a philosophy test. "Sixty?" she tries.

The cop makes a soft sort of grunting noise. "More like eighty."

"Oh, no!"

"We didn't realize," I say pleadingly now, but he ignores me.

"And who does this belong to?" He lifts the bikini top from the driver's-side mirror, lets it dangle from his pinky finger.

"That would be mine, sir."

"And why was it on the mirror?"

"I was trying to dry it out?"

The radio on the cop's belt emits a bleep of static, and he suddenly seems to lose patience. "You," he points his flashlight at Lila. "Out of the car!" he barks.

We exchange glances, and inconceivably, Lila winks at me before easing herself gracefully out of the car. The edges of her sarong part ways, one bare flash of thigh, but I notice the cop's eyes are still as hard as needles. Lila lets the door fall not completely shut, and it emits a constant dinging noise in protest. I lick my lips repeatedly, but they feel paper-dry.

"Walk this white line, right here on the side of the road. One foot in front of the other." His voice is heavily bored.

Lila steps out, pauses, looks over her shoulder. "Can I start now?"

He nods, and I watch her place one foot in front of the other, perfectly, her hips swinging just slightly side to side. She seems ready to walk away into the falling dark, her sarong a swaying red beacon, but then the cop calls out to her.

"Stop. Turn. Walk back to me."

Lila follows each of these commands, equally gracefully, and now I can see that her toes are pointed as if she were a gymnast on a balance beam. I steal another look at the monolith. He still does not seem impressed.

"Hold out your arms, touch your nose three times with your first finger of each hand."

"Alternating or consecutively?" Lila asks, and I inch farther down in my seat. A car whooshes by us, then another, and when there is only a clip of taillights, the cop speaks again.

"You think this is funny? You want me to take you down to the station?"

"No, sir," Lila says, and now her voice is milk-white meek. She touches her nose obediently, evenly.

"License and registration, please."

Lila slides back in beside me, and after a short search in the glove compartment, hands him a small square of paper and her license. He wheels back to his car.

I close my eyes. The flashing lights are sweeping, pounding through my skull. "Nice performance," I murmur. "Maybe you should have taken a bow."

Next to me, in the growing darkness, I hear her give a small spurt of a laugh. And suddenly, I am laughing too. The snorting kind of laugh that starts in hiccupping ripples. The kind of laughing Ollie and I used to regularly engage in during long, endless dinners with my father's business associates when we used to have to wear our best clothes and manners and listen to everything the adults said. The kind of laughing I haven't done with anyone since Ollie.

"Stop, stop it!" I finally hiss, twisting in my seat. "He's coming back."

"All clear, Miss Harris. I'm writing you out a warning this time." He scribbles something on a slip, tears it off, hands it to her.

"Thank you so much." She holds the paper over the lower half of her face, and I am immediately reminded of paintings of those Venetian courtesans, half their faces hidden by fantastical masks, their eyebrows arched over mocking eyes.

"Don't let me catch you speeding again."

"I won't," she promises earnestly, the corner of her mouth clamping down, and unobtrusively, I flick my thumb and forefinger hard against her thigh.

"I won't let her, either," I add, and the cop stares at me for one stark second. All the laughter fizzles flat in my throat. Without another word, he leaves us. His car door slams shut, but he waits until Lila starts the engine again and merges back onto the road, carefully signaling first even though the highway is empty for the moment.

He follows us to the next exit, and I think he's going to continue following us, but at the last second, he veers past, and we are heading toward the exit ramp.

"That was Fryin' Ryan's father," Lila says. Then she gives me a wicked grin. "Want to learn to drive?"

Lila eases the car into the deserted parking lot of the high school and cuts the engine. She reaches into her purse, pulls out a tube of lip gloss, uncaps it. I look at the rows of dark classroom windows. "I don't know," I say, my voice refusing to hold steady. I pick up an old gum wrapper in the cup holder, begin shredding it into tiny scraps.

Lila outlines her lips with careful strokes, checking her progress in the rearview mirror. "My mom was all, like, 'When you get your license, don't think you'll be taking the car out by yourself. I'm not putting a half ton of steel in some dumb teenager's hands. It's a weapon.'" She snorts. "That lasted about six hours, until she figured out that she could send me to the grocery store and to pick up my little brothers at their soccer practice. Besides, my dad had already given me this car, so what could she do?"

"Your dad gave you this car?" I ask. I let my hand dangle out the window. I try to imagine what that moment must have been like. "My dad gave me a bike."

Lila snorts. "Yeah, but your dad stuck around. This car was my dad's baby. He bought it at some car auction years ago. He always wanted a classic Beetle. I wanted him to get a new one and, of course, we couldn't afford *that*."

"This is a true California car," I muse.

"This car was probably the start of all the trouble between them. He rebuilt the engine. Then when he gave it to me, I knew he was going for good. Signed the deed over. Now it's mine." She gives the dashboard a thump.

"And your mom didn't make you sell it?"

"It's more than thirty years old, it's got a hundred and twenty thousand miles on it. She wasn't going to get much. She did try," Lila adds. "She's a wackjob anyway. I think she should have stopped after two kids. It's about all she can handle. You're lucky to be an only child."

I stare at the edge of the field that borders the parking lot, at the shadows welling beyond the circle of feeble light cast by the streetlamp. "I'm not," I say so softly that I think she doesn't hear me.

But she asks after a minute, "So, what happened?" in the same dry, nonchalant tone that she always uses.

I don't know what I expected. "My brother. My twin brother, Ollie. He died in a car accident."

"Oh," Lila says simply, and snaps the top back on her tube of lip gloss. She looks at me, says briefly, "I'm sorry."

I shrug. "That's why she won't let me take the Driver's Ed class."

Lila nods. "Your dad?"

I shrug again. "No way he's going against her."

I watch as she dabs the corner of her mouth. "That's easy," she pronounces after a minute. "Sign the permission slip yourself then."

"What?"

"I've faked my mom's signature tons of times."

"But–"

"The class is on Tuesday afternoons, right? Just say you're at my house for our weekly study session or some crap like that. Look," Lila explains, her tone shot through with reason, "once you've taken the class, it'll make your position that much stronger."

"What if I fail the class?"

She gives me a bewildered look. "No one fails that class. And I mean *no one*. Not even the losers. And if I teach you the basics. . ."

I begin to pick the tiny silver shreds of gum wrapper off my jeans. "You know that's illegal."

"Ooh!" Lila says, and rolls her eyes skyward. "Stop scaring me."

❧

"Comfy?" Lila asks.

I wriggle around in the cracked leather seat, glide my fingers over the dashboard, fiddling with knobs and buttons. Through all this, Lila waits with a patient expression on her face. "Ready," I say at last.

"Okay. First thing when you get into someone else's car. Make sure the driver's seat is positioned where you want it and that all the mirrors are right." Her voice has gotten suddenly deeper, and she is speaking crisply, enunciating her syllables. I try not to giggle.

I glance at each side-mirror, spend a long time deciding that yes, I can see clearly out of them. Then I put my hand up to the rearview mirror and adjust it carefully.

From the darkness of the backseat, my brother's eyes stare accusingly at me. He is curled into a tight ball, his arms locked around his knees.

And suddenly, I feel like I am going to throw up.

"I can't do this," I say, and my voice is shaking, sliding a little.

"Here, let me see," Lila says, leans across the divider, and pushes the mirror back and forth. "Sometimes it really sticks." The sweet smell of her shampoo drifts over, and I breathe in deeply, closing my eyes. When I open them again, my brother is gone.

"Sadie," Lila says, watching me, and her voice is unexpectedly gentle. "It's going to be okay."

I manage to smile at her, and then I put my hands back on the wheel.

"Now turn the key in the ignition." She waits a beat. "Okay, it's not going to bite you. You can turn it a little hard–there you go!"

The car jerks to life underneath me, and I can't help it, I feel a spurt of happiness.

"Now, this part is a little tricky," Lila continues. "Press in the clutch, yeah, that farthest pedal on the left–"

"Like that?"

"Yeah, like that. Take the gear shift, put it into reverse, no, that's first, here." She wraps her hand around mine, and our closed fists jam backward. The car gives a little judder. "Now, slowly, slowly, let go of the clutch and push in the gas pedal."

I lift my toes first, then the arch of my foot, then my heel, as slowly as possible, all the while pressing in tiny increments on the gas. The engine shudders, stiffens, bucks once. Dies.

"Take two," Lila says, her voice neutral.

Chapter Ten

What I know.

We were twelve. I was down in the courtyard just as the sun was setting, having gotten an irresistible urge to paint the lemon tree caught against the last golden red wedge of sky. I was setting up spotlights, angling them carefully across my easel, when you scuffed into my line of vision.

You walked in circles around me, watching me adjust and readjust lights until I got the perfect tilt. I wasn't talking to you. I was still mad from our fight earlier that afternoon. "Come on," you pleaded with me. "Let's go down to Bullet Beach and swim. You can paint later."

"I'm drawing first," I couldn't help pointing out, still not looking at you. I didn't need to, to know what you looked like. Like me. But not so much like me anymore, it seemed. Your hollow bones were still forming sharp angles, while mine had begun to soften and grow heavy.

"Then just come down to the beach with me. You can draw the ocean," you added, and I could feel you flashing a smile at me that was a direct echo of my own.

Night swimming was expressly forbidden. So, of course, it held a lot of appeal. I hesitated, could feel myself about to make the motions to pack up my charcoals. But then I remembered that you had stolen my glass calligraphy pen, the one Dad had brought me from Italy. You wouldn't give it back, and when I got mad and screamed at you, so sure that you would break it, Mom took your side and sent me to my room.

Besides, I was waiting for Chris Jackson to call me. He had said he was going to earlier that day in school. So now I shook my head. "I don't feel like it, Ollie," I said, and turned back to my easel and the clean white sheet of paper. "And anyway," I added, the edges of my voice curling up with just the right amount of scorn, "it's impossible to draw the ocean."

After a while, I noticed your absence. Maybe it was the gate squeaking slightly in the breeze that was coming off the ocean. You had a bad habit of leaving it open, and our mother was always yelling at both of us for that. I'm not sure how much time passed. The phone had rung once, but although I had made it into the house before the second ring, the call was for Mom. I had filled three pages with sketches before mixing a palette full of paint and switching to canvas.

And then I heard you shouting.

I was mesmerized by the way the light poured like liquid from my brush, and it took a while before the block of sound, hammering over and over at my ears, resolved itself into a word.

"Lycee, Lycee, Lycee!" you were calling. "Lycee, come!" Lycee, our ten-year-old boxer, was always trying to follow you wherever you went. "Sadie!" you screamed from somewhere hidden, somewhere beyond me. "Sadie, help me! Lycee's gotten out!"

"Call her back!" I yelled over my shoulder, swirling the canvas with creamy apricot-gold. Lycee got out every so often, and I knew that you worried she would get lost, but she always came back, her ears and tail drooping, her tongue sliding wet pink from her slack jaw. Usually, she went to visit the Larsons down the hill, where I know they fed her scraps and bones from dinner.

There was a silence, then it was as if all sound speeded up and tore through the courtyard at an impossible pace before fusing into a blaring howl, inhuman.

I turned so fast that the back of my hand scraped across wet canvas, and then I was flying down the short driveway. I slammed through the still open gate.

This is what I saw.

You. Lying in a flood of headlights. Your face so still and sweet and calm, your eyes closed. This picture came to me in pieces, pieces that broke and reformed and broke again. Voices screaming and doors slamming. The silent silver jaguar of the Larsons' car, its mouth frozen in a snarl, as if warning us to keep away from you. And a cloud of those fluttering angel-blue moths that always come out in the evening.

I slapped the pavement next to your head. *"Get up, get up, get up, Ollie! I'll draw the ocean for you, I'll draw the ocean, I'll draw it for you! Get up!"* And then when you didn't answer, I screamed your name over and over and over until someone grasped my elbows, pulled me, stumbling, through darkness.

❧

When I woke, you were sitting by my bed, your knees just brushing the edge of the white coverlet. I lurched up so fast, held out my hands to yours, which were just out of reach. I must have made a noise, called out. You grinned at me, put your finger to your lips, and winked. When the door opened and the wedge of light widened, you vanished.

We were twelve. Part of me will be twelve forever. All of you will be.

Chapter Eleven

"Go, Pioneer!" Erica screams next to me. As if this is the signal, the rest of the crowd all around me begins hooting and stomping their feet as our football team jaunts out onto the field. The bleachers rumble and quiver with the commotion.

"Go, Pioneer, go!" Erica shrieks again, and Lila looks up briefly.

"I think they heard you," Lila says mildly enough. I watch Erica's cheeks pinken in the cold air. I sit down, and after a second, so does Erica. A shrill whistle blows, and below, Coach Vesecki huddles on the sidelines with a player, then sends him onto the field with a slap to the guy's well-padded shoulder.

"There's Travis," Erica says to the air. I wonder how she can tell who anyone is under the helmets until she adds casually, "He's number twenty-seven. That's his lucky number. He told me."

Christie and Ruth come back from the concession stand, bearing buckets of popcorn and steaming paper cups. "They ran out of Coke," Ruth huffs as she climbs the bleachers toward us. She hands me a cup. "Hot chocolate," she says.

I take a sip of the steaming cocoa-flavored water, and the roof of my mouth immediately feels fuzzy. I hand the cup to Lila.

It's the first game of the season, and Erica insisted that we all had to go for team support. It's also a home game, which Erica has explained to me is good because the players feel much better on their own turf. To which Lila snorted and pointed out that it doesn't matter how much better the team *feels,* since they will invariably lose.

I watch as the Pioneer Mountain players in their red-and-white uniforms pile onto a bunch of other players dressed in blue and green. Then the referee blows his whistle, and either Coach Vesecki or the other coach, who looks remarkably like Coach Vesecki, waves his arms and stomps out onto the field. Sometimes, due to some mysterious signal, a red-and-white player or a blue-and-green player will trot off to the sidelines. Sometimes they don't return; instead, they seem to be replaced by identical players. Then they all pile onto each other again and the gigantic clock ticks away the seconds and sometimes freezes for no reason that I can see.

I shift on the hard metal bleachers, discover that my right foot has gone to sleep and try to revive it. Ruth is text-messaging on her cell phone, Christie keeps craning her neck left and right and bursting into bouts of frantic waving. Lila is staring out at the field with every appearance of interest, but her lips are moving and, every once in a while, she glances down at the notes in her hand. She has been running lines all week with me and Erica.

"So, what's happening to–" I begin, looking at Erica.

"Oh my God!" she says. "Oh my God, oh my God, he's going to do it–"

I lean forward as player number 27 struggles free from the pack and runs down the field, weaving some complicated pattern. Erica grabs my arm, pulls me to my feet.

"Touchdown by Hartshorn!" the announcer blares out, and I recognize Mr. Hutchinson's enthusiastic voice. Our side of the bleachers erupts.

Even Lila is standing now. "Not bad," she says approvingly, before sitting back down and pulling a tightly folded newspaper from her bag. She disappears behind it. I watch the field, expecting something interesting to happen again, but after a while, I give up and start reading over Lila's shoulder.

Auditioning for **"Soldier's Wife."** All roles open. Non equity.

National Model Search. Agencies from all around the world will be in the Plaza Hotel on Saturday, October 14, and Sunday, October 15th, for the 5th Annual National Model Search.

Reality TV: 'Love Around the World' Are you between the ages of 22 and 28? Do you have that "special something"? Are you the next big thing? Then come and show us what you've got on Monday, October 16th at 2:00, Studio 18, 445 Broadway.

"You do have that special something," I murmur.

She rattles one corner of her paper at me, smiles. "That's for a reality TV show. Not my style."

I study the ads with her again. Each week, Lila pores over her copy of *Backstage*, her fingers smudged with the cheap black ink. "What about that one?" I say, pointing with my knuckle.

Lila reads, "Seeking Female, tall, dark hair, full nudity, no pay." She whistles. "Wow, sign me up!"

"What are you guys looking at?" Erica says, leans over me. "Oh, that. You're always looking at that paper."

"Yes, because it's a weekly. A *weekly* paper. Therefore, it changes from week to week."

Erica snorts. "Is there ever anything good in there?"

Lila shrugs. "Sometimes. Good plays. Independent movies."

"Yeah, but do you ever go to any of the auditions? You've been reading that paper for, like, what, a year now?" Erica turns back to the game, leans forward. “Oh my God, Travis is on fire today!” She flings out her arm, and I watch as Travis muscles his way down the field again in what seems like a replay of three minutes ago. “Go, go, go!” Erica urges.

“Touchdown, again by Hartshorn!” Mr. Hutchinson shouts. Erica hops up and down, throws her arms around Ruth, knocking her cell phone out of her hand. As they scramble to find it in the sea of stomping feet, I look back at Lila.

She has shielded her face completely with the paper. All I can see is the top of her head.

❧

Despite two spectacular touchdowns by Travis, it's clear that Pioneer Mountain is going to lose. No one seems surprised about this, except for Erica. “If only they had a better defense. How can Travis do his job as the tight end, unless the defense–”

“Did you take a Football 101 course over the summer?” Lila inquires.

Erica shrugs. “I just like the game.”

“Maybe you should be a cheerleader then. I mean, you're only missing the pom-poms.”

I watch as Ruth draws in a breath, exchanges a wide-eyed look with Christie. Then they huddle closer to Erica.

“You know I tried out for the cheerleaders last year,” Erica says, staring out at the field. “You know I didn't get in.”

I look up at the very top bleacher, where Ollie is waving one hand at me. I look back at Lila, raise my eyebrows. She shrugs, tries to fold her paper back along its original lines.

“At least I tried out for something,” Erica adds.

“You're right, Erica,” Lila says quietly, almost too quietly, but Erica turns to her in obvious surprise.

❧

No sooner do I shut the front door, than I hear, "Is that you, Bug?" from my father.

"That's me," I call back, clanking hangers together in the hall closet as I try to hang up my jacket.

A minute later, my father enters the kitchen, holding his newspaper in one hand. "Well, it looks like we're on our own tonight."

Behind me, I hear a whole pile of coats slither to the floor.

"Mom's at her first class tonight."

"Oh, right. I forgot that started." Marie had convinced my mother to take a Women in Literature class at the local community college, and my mother, reluctant at first, had gotten so excited that I had gone with her to the bookstore downtown to pick out the copies of the books they would be reading.

"Your mother, uh, prepared dinner for us. She left a casserole," my father says as I finish hanging up the last of the coats. I shut the closet door carefully, study his slightly mournful face. He is standing at the counter, peeling back a corner of shiny aluminum foil.

I pull a Coke from the fridge, come to stand beside him. We stare down at withered green-bean tips poking their way out of a soggy-looking crust. "What is it?" I ask at last.

"A lasagna."

I stare at it some more. "That doesn't look right. Lasagna doesn't have green beans."

My father clears his throat. "I think she said it was *like* a lasagna. With green beans. And some other . . . things."

"I think I'm not hungry." I pick up my bag, begin to exit the kitchen.

"Not even for pizza?" my father asks hopefully behind me.

I stop. "But then she'll see the box. Dad, her feelings," I remind him.

Slowly, my father unwraps the rest of the casserole, then opens the cupboard where we keep the plates and gazes into its depths as if he can't remember what he wanted in the first place.

"But . . . we could make pancakes," I offer. "And wash up everything afterward."

Chapter Twelve

On the Monday morning after the football game, Travis Hartshorn is walking toward me, and I decide it might not be that hard to fall in love. He is wearing a white long-sleeved shirt with a sky blue T-shirt layered over it, and his jeans have that worn and faded look. He moves down the hall like he moved down the field, with confidence and surety, greeting just about everyone in the whole place. His blond hair is cut close to his head, and his cheeks are flushed as if he just came in from outdoors.

The girl in front of me stops abruptly, squealing, "Ohmigod!" She waves her cell phone above her head, but I never do figure out why she is so excited. I am too busy chasing down my extra set of charcoals, now scattered on the hallway floor, being smashed into dust beneath people's feet.

I kneel, scrabbling to pick up as many whole pieces as I can, and when I look up, Travis is gone.

"Why are you on the floor?" Lila glides to a stop next to me, and I am vaguely aware that she has extended her hand. I allow her to pull me up.

"So," I begin casually. "Travis Hartshorn. What's he like?"

"Oh. No. Not you, too." Her voice is grimly resigned.

She shakes her head at me. I let her turn me so I am facing the right direction. "What class have you got now?"

"Chemistry," I murmur, and can't understand why she starts laughing.

❧

At lunch, I wander into the Student Center, and then my feet fail to move any more. Travis Hartshorn is sitting at one end of my table. Erica is perched at his right side, talking with her hands, her face lively. Lila is sitting on his left.

I thought about him, all through Chemistry, as I tried to concentrate on changing the color of the contents of my glass beaker from red to green. But no brilliant schemes came to mind, and staring at the murky brown contents of my beaker, I could only conclude that chemistry can't be forced.

I examine the far wall, which bears a fresh batch of jaunty red letters:

IF YOU CAN DREAM—AND NOT MAKE DREAMS YOUR MASTER;
IF YOU CAN THINK—AND NOT MAKE THOUGHTS YOUR AIM

The custodians seem to have abandoned the job of clearing away these new lines. A ladder and bucket stand unattended for the moment.

"Sadie," Lila calls, waves to me. Pinning my eyes to her face as if it is my anchor, I let myself be tugged in. "I was just telling Travis about our little brush with the law."

I smile weakly. "Yeah. That was pretty . . . wild." For some reason, the chair I have chosen is stuck under the table. I pull futilely at it.

"Getting arrested isn't that intelligent," Erica says, and her voice is like a draught of sweet, pure poison.

Travis leans over and yanks the chair free for me. The base of it slams into my shin, but I smile anyway. "Thanks," I murmur.

"No problem," he says, his voice easy and low.

I sit, my back very straight and tall, and find myself saying,

"I agree, Erica. Which is why you will have to admit that we were pretty intelligent to *not* get arrested." The words feel like they are hanging in the air, and I picture them bullfighter red.

Lila gives me a nod, and is quick to add, "Sadie saved the day."

"I did not," I protest. But not very loudly.

"She just *yes, sir'*d and *no, sir'*d him and batted her eyelashes, and he couldn't help but let us go with only a warning." The corners of Lila's eyelids crinkle in an almost-secret wink.

But looking at Erica's set face, I realize it is not secret enough, and so I ask quickly, "So, who keeps doing that?" I gesture at the wall.

"Maybe it's for the poetry club," Erica shrugs. "Who knows?" She takes her iPod out of her bag.

Lila studies the lines for a minute as if committing them to memory, but she remains silent.

And just when I think that conversation is going nowhere, Travis adds, "That stuff was in the locker room last week."

"The same words?" I ask.

He studies the wall. "Different." He looks thoughtful. "And once in my Calculus class. On the blackboard." Then he looks at me. "So, you're new here, huh?"

I nod. Something smashes into my ankle, and I follow up this witty response with, "Yes, I moved here from California."

"California? Wow. L.A.?"

"No. Sort of north."

"Sort of north?" he repeats, and for one horrible second, I think he is imitating me, but then I decide he is not.

"Livingston. A small town."

"Oh, yeah? I'm looking at UCLA for school."

"That's great," I say eagerly, then try to tone it down a little. "That's supposed to be a good school." Travis is nodding, looking at me so intently, and I notice that his eyes are two shades darker than the blue of his T-shirt. I blurt out, "I have pictures."

"Of UCLA?" Now Travis is looking confused.

Erica gives a tinkling sort of laugh, like breaking crystal.

"No, just . . . California," I mumble, resisting the urge to cover the tips of my ears.

"I bet they're amazing," Lila interjects, turns to Travis. "Sadie's an artist."

He smiles at me.

❧

"Spill," I say to Lila as we walk out into the October sunshine together.

She inclines her head toward me, adjusts her large, wrap-around sunglasses. The frames are wide and tilt upward at the corners, giving her a catlike look.

"Spill?" she echoes, the word acquiring edges in her precise pitch.

"Everything you know about Travis Hartshorn."

We walk across the courtyard, skirt the outlines of a hop-scotch game. A much younger girl bounces through the squares to the accompaniment of some complicated hand-clapping rhythm game. "Josie, Josie, you're so fine, just don't step on the purple line. Josie, Josie, you're so fine, just don't–oooh!" Their squeaky-sweet voices shade into a collective shrill of laughter as Josie reaches the ten, overplants her feet, and tumbles out of bounds.

"Travis Hartshorn," Lila muses. "Everything. Okay. One time, in second grade, he called me retarded, so when we were at recess, I threw sand at him in the sandbox, and then when the teacher came over, I started crying and saying–"

"Lila."

She stops and looks at me, her mouth quirked upward. "Okay, okay, okay. Travis Hartshorn." We head toward the row of cars in the parking lot. "He's a football player. But a nice one. Not one of your usual meatheads. He dates . . . mainly cheerleaders. I don't know why, really. He had a girlfriend for a while who went to St. Vincent's. They broke up this summer, and since school started, everyone's after him."

I stop in my tracks, but Lila doesn't, so I hurry to catch up with her. I can't, can't, can't ask. I ask. "Including you?"

And am rewarded by Lila's snort. "Not likely."

I pause, frown. "Why not? He's so . . ."

"So what? So *what*, Caldwell?"

I shrug. "I don't know."

"Too much white bread for me."

"White *bread*?"

"You know, white Wonder bread–vanilla, plain, boring."

"How can you *say* that?"

"How can you *say* that?" Lila mimics me almost perfectly. "Hey, where's your driver, by the way? Late?"

I stop again. After a few seconds, she wheels. We look at each other for a minute, or at least I think she is looking at me. It's hard to tell behind her ridiculous Jackie O sunglasses. The breeze shifts the branches of trees over our heads, and a few leaves, splotched with early color, come quivering down.

She holds up both hands. "You really want him?"

"It doesn't matter." My right shoulder is beginning to ache, so I switch my backpack to my left one. "He'll never look at me."

Lila appraises me. "You have the dark-horse factor going for you."

"Now I'm a horse?" I smile.

"You know what I mean." She looks up at the sky briefly, then back at me. "He's not interested in Erica, that's for sure."

"How do you know?"

"I can just tell."

"But Erica really likes him."

"C'est la vie," Lila says, without much mercy in her voice. Then she looks at me. "Don't let Erica's liking him stop you. Erica wouldn't let it stop her."

❧

"There's a party this weekend," Lila announces as I sit down beside her the next morning.

I scoot my knees to fit under the desk and wonder suddenly, if he had lived, who would be taller right now, Ollie or me?

"At Travis's house," Lila adds. I promptly knock both my notebook and my copy of *Romeo and Juliet* off my desk.

"Really?" I squeak, scrambling to pick up my books.

"Really. On Saturday."

"Where are his parents?" I manage not to bump my head on the corner of my desk as I straighten up.

Lila smiles at me. "I like your thinking. They're in Europe for two weeks." She yawns, flashing perfect pearls for teeth, then offers casually, "Want to go?"

I touch the corner of my book, its spine frayed and inked with pen lines. "Was I invited? Because maybe he doesn't want just anyone–"

"For your information, Travis stopped me in the hallway to tell me about the party, and he specifically said, 'Hey, bring your friend, the new girl, from California.' So new girl from California, I repeat, do you want to go?"

Chapter Thirteen

"Sadie," my mother says hesitantly, alighting in the doorway of my room. I look at her in the mirror of my dresser, then turn, leaning against the heavy oak furniture. There is a small gouge in one of the drawers, which is why my father was able to bargain down the price at another tag sale last week.

"I have droopy eyelashes," I announce.

My mother blinks a little. "You don't–" she begins with a smile.

"I do," I insist. "Don't try to deny it." I stare at the mirror again, at my puffy eyelids, which I have now pinched numerous times with my mother's eyelash curler. "Why, why, am I cursed with this? Ollie had perfect eyelashes."

My mother has gone very still, and I think that she will retreat. I watch the struggle play over her face before she steps forward, coming all the way into the room.

"Wasted on a boy," I add, hoping this is not too much for her. She smiles again, slower this time, but unhooks the eyelash curler from my fingers.

"Hold still," she murmurs, concentrating. "Tell me if I'm hurting you."

"You're not." I resist the urge to blink as one eye begins to water.

"There." She leans back, examines me critically. "Where's your mascara?"

I hand her the narrow tube and she frowns at it. "This is too black. You need a brown-black, to go better with your eyes."

I shrug. "I like it."

"Okay," she concedes, unscrews the top, dips the wand, and proceeds to dab at my eyelashes. She leans back. "Lovely."

I turn and blink at the mirror, lean closer, putting up one finger to dab away a smudge. "Thanks," I say, grin up at her.

"Sadie, I know this is silly, but I just wanted to talk to you about . . ."

I am not sure how to help her.

"To talk to you about boys," she finishes, and holds up one hand as I groan, flop onto my bed. "I know, I know, you know everything already, it seems. I just want to make sure we're on the same page."

I give my mother a look. This definitely does not sound like her. "Have you been reading some manual?" I ask half seriously.

She comes to sit on the bed with me. "I never had this kind of talk with my own mother."

"Lucky you," I murmur, and she swats at my knee lightly.

"The point is, I wanted to. I want you to be able to talk to me about . . . things."

"Things?"

"Things. About what you may be feeling."

"Feeling?"

"Yes, feeling. About anything."

Like Ollie? I want to ask, but don't.

"About boys," she adds.

"Okay."

She seems to be waiting.

"Okay," I try again. "I will. If I'm feeling anything, I'll come talk to you about it."

She sighs. "I didn't know if we would ever have this talk. You seemed so . . . content in your own world." She makes a circling motion with her hand. "Painting and everything." She bites down on the last word, and I wonder if she is about to start crying. "But I suppose you're just a late bloomer, is all." Then she turns to me with a fierce look. "And there's nothing wrong with that."

I nod, not sure if I am required to give any more of a response.

"I know boys today can put a lot of pressure on girls."

I knew it. The manual talk. Lila said her mother gave her this talk when she was twelve. Apparently, she was not considered a late bloomer.

"If you like a boy, make sure he's worthy of you."

I really don't want to prolong this, but I can't help asking, "How do I do that?"

My mother jumps on this. "Make sure that he's nice, smart, respectful." She ticks these items off on her fingers like she's making a shopping list. "Pay attention to how he is with his friends. Is he different? Also, make sure he listens to you, asks you about yourself." Her fingers spread apart. "Most important. Ask yourself if you like who you are when you're with him."

"That's all?"

But she seems to be on her own track now. "I always thought . . ." She sighs again and presses one knuckle into her eye. "I always thought that . . . he would be there to look out for you."

I slip my hand into hers. I want so badly to tell her that Ollie *does* look out for me. In his own way. But I can't. So I concentrate on deciding what color I would paint the air between us. Soft gray flecked with blue.

After a minute, she manages a smile. "Let's not ruin your mascara." She stands, looks around my room, focuses on a pile of painting smocks that have fallen in a crumpled heap by my desk. "You know, you do have a perfectly functional closet."

"I like to throw my clothes on the floor. That way I can see all my options at once."

She nods. "Anyway, your father is downstairs. He'll give you a ride to the party."

I look steadily at her. "Mom," I begin. "Lila is picking me up at nine. I thought we got past this already."

"I . . ."

"I cannot have Dad give me a ride to the party. Do you know how weird that would look?"

My mother blinks. "No. Why would it be weird? He's not going to come in and talk to the parents or anything." Then she narrows in on me. "This boy's parents are going to be there, right?"

"Yes," I say, my voice crisp and sure and even.

My mother touches a fallen tube of lipstick on my dresser, rights it. "I think your father wants to talk to you. He hasn't seen you in two weeks. And he misses you," she adds. My father has been in Chile helping to open a start-up division of the bank there.

"Okay. Can he just give me a ride to Lila's house then?"

She hesitates.

"Mom. Lila's a very good driver. Sometimes she won't even let us listen to music in the car because she says she needs to concentrate."

My mother's shoulders melt downward. "Okay," she says, and there is defeat in her voice.

Suddenly, I wish we could go back to the talk about how I am a late bloomer.

❧

"Listen, Sadie," my father begins as we sit in the driveway. "Your mother tells me you're going to a party at some boy's house."

"Not you, too," I protest, clicking my seat belt into place.

My father guides the car out of the driveway, lightly taps the horn once. The silhouette behind the kitchen curtains raises a hand in a brief ripple of a wave.

"No, no," he says, but then continues. "I just want to say four things."

"*Four* things?"

"Yes. Four." My father clears his throat. I wonder if he and my mother have rehearsed this privately.

"Respect yourself. Respect others. Know your limits." He pauses, ticks on the blinker. "And have fun."

"Um . . . thanks. Turn here." I peer at the directions Lila gave me over the phone, her voice definitely amused after I told her my father was giving me a ride to her house. "She said the third house on the left." I spot the Beetle in the driveway. Its engine is already running. "That's it." I lean forward a little. "Thanks, Daddy," I say, and kiss him on the cheek. "Listen. Do you think you could talk to Mom again about letting me learn to drive? I mean, I'm eligible for my driver's permit and all."

My father takes off his glasses and presses the bridge of his nose between two fingers. "I can try, Sadie. Your mother has some very . . . definite ideas."

"I know. But I'm past the age where everyone learns to drive. I've been sixteen for *five* months already. That's practically sixteen and a half."

"My, you're old," my father says mildly.

"Please?" And without waiting for him to answer, I unfasten my belt, grab my purse.

"Listen, Sadie," he says, and now his voice is more urgent. "Call if you need anything. A ride home or . . . anything."

"Okay." I open the door.

"You have the cell phone."

I pat the hard lump in my purse. "Right here."

"Have fun," my father says as I climb out of the car. It sounds like a warning.

❧

Lila is driving carefully tonight, promptly using her turn signal and generally following the speed limits. I glance sideways at her, but she seems to be concentrating. I touch the tip of my tongue to my lower lip, exploring the flavor of the pale pink gloss she had insisted I try.

"Are you and Erica really friends?" I ask finally.

"In a fashion. As much as anyone is friends with anyone."

I lean back a little, feeling the unfamiliar dangle and sway of the silver hoops that Lila had also pressed on me, insisting that they went with the seven sterling silver bangles my mother had given me the day we moved from California. I had jingled and jangled them over and over on the plane, until my father had twitched his newspaper aside, clapped one hand over my arm.

Now I slide the bangles up and down my arm, listening to their musical chatter. "It doesn't seem like you like her," I venture at last.

Lila lowers the volume on the radio. "I've been friends with Erica since fourth grade. We used to be closer. We used to talk about things. *Real* things. I don't know. Maybe I'm just tired of seeing her get everything she wants handed to her on a silver platter."

I wonder what it is that Lila wants and can't have. But before I have time to figure out a way to ask her, we are sweeping up a long, arching driveway flanked with stone columns. "Speaking of silver platters," Lila mutters as she navigates a place to park next to what seems like dozens of Saabs and Jeeps and Audis.

Lila fumbles through her purse. At first, I think she is looking for more lip gloss, but instead she hands me a tiny flask. "Have a sip." She grins. "It'll help you relax."

I unscrew the cap, inhale the strong scent of alcohol.

When Ollie and I were little, we used to sneak into the shade-drawn dining room that was used only for special occasions and examine all the cut-glass decanters lined up on the sideboard. I loved to run my fingers over all the containers full of amber- and peach- and apricot-colored liquids while Ollie told me stories about the magical powers these potions granted to the one who was brave enough to drink.

I tip the flask cautiously toward my lips, let the liquid spark on my tongue, and pass it to Lila. She takes a long, practiced swig, tucks it away in her purse. "I hope there's some good food, at least," she murmurs as we get out of the car.

Chapter Fourteen ❧

"This music sucks," Lila announces ten seconds after we walk through the front door. I can barely hear her. The bass, way too loud, is jamming up inside my throat.

"Do you know where the bathroom is?"

"What?"

"Bathroom!" I scream, and she shakes her head. I stare at a bunch of mostly empty beer bottles scattered on a walnut bookshelf. They've got to be leaving rings, and I can imagine my mother's look of horror that someone would do that to *furniture*.

"I'll come with you," Lila offers after a moment, and I am grateful. Somehow she manages to lead me through the crush of people, until we find ourselves standing outside a small door. We try the knob, find it locked tight, and wait until a guy I vaguely recognize from Chemistry class comes stumbling out.

"Thanks," he says to the air somewhere between our shoulders.

"Go ahead," I say, sweep my arm into a magnanimous gesture, and Lila gives me a wry look before closing the door behind her. Left alone, I study all the people spilling in and out of the hallway. At one point, I think I see Erica's frizzy head of hair bobbing along, but I turn away quickly. The bathroom door opens.

"Is that Poodle?" Lila asks, close to my ear. She has taken to calling Erica that ever since she freed her hair from the Barbados braids. I think her hair, falling kinky-curled to her shoulders, looks really pretty.

"Maybe," I say now.

"Let's go say hi."

"Do we have to?"

Lila gives me an exasperated look. "Well, where she is, is where you'll find Travis. Haven't you noticed the girl is glued to his hip?"

"We can find them later," I venture, swallowing hard.

"Caldwell, if you want him, you're going to have to give him some sign, some indication. In case you hadn't noticed, guys are kind of clueless. So let's go say hi."

A short girl dressed in a lacy white tank top and jeans feels her way down the wall like a blind person until she passes me. She slams the door closed, but I can still hear the loud and unmistakable sounds of her being sick. I decide I don't need the bathroom that urgently anyway.

❧

When we finally do find Travis upstairs, he is sitting with a small circle of people in what looks like a guest bedroom. Erica is curled into his side and her eyes glint at me, but I ignore the warning.

"Sadie," Travis says, disentangles himself, stands. "Sadie and Lila," he announces to the room. "I'm so glad you guys made it."

"Hey, Travis," Lila says coolly, nods at a few other people, goes to sit in the vacant space that he has left. She leans over Erica, runs one finger down her wrist. "That's really pretty," I hear her say. "Temporary, right? Would you do one for me later?"

I watch Erica struggle, nod, then all of a sudden, she is hugging Lila and appears to be crying on her shoulder.

"Sadie," Travis says again, and I jolt back to him. "Would you like a drink or anything?"

"I'm fine right now," I say. "Thanks."

"You're sure? How about the tour?"

"Okay." I nod rapidly, my eyes stuck on the pocket of his shirt.

"Guys, wait up five minutes for us. I'm just going to give Sadie the tour."

One of the boys wolf whistles and won't stop until Lila says coldly, "Oh, really, James, what are you, eleven?" Travis closes the door behind us and we are alone. In a house full of people.

"So," he says, "this is the–"

"Hallway," I supply, wondering if guys get nervous. I hope they do. I walk a few steps ahead of him, pausing to examine the paintings in their gilded frames. There are a lot of seascapes and lighthouses and fields of grass with flowers. "These are nice," I add, wishing that I didn't feel like each word was a struggle to produce.

"Yeah? My mom's really into art."

"I like art," I find myself saying, then worry that will make him link me to his mother. "Sometimes." Then I remember my own mother's advice. "A lot. I really like it a lot."

Travis nods, looking slightly confused now. I smile. "The rest of the tour?"

"This way," he says. We pass room after room of majestic dark colonial furniture and muted jewel-tone rugs.

"Wow," I say finally as we wind down the back staircase. "How many brothers and sisters do you have?"

"None. I'm an only child."

"Wow," I say again, trying to think of something else besides *wow.*

He looks down at me, brushes back a strand of my hair, and I go very still. "So, a drink for you?" he asks softly, and I nod. "Beer's okay?"

"Sure." I try to think of a good brand of beer, a brand that will signify that I know my beer, but Travis doesn't ask as he walks over to a cooler resting on the kitchen table. Some guy in a paisley-patterned smoking jacket slaps him on the back, and Travis turns, grins, listens intently, before shaking his head. He points a beer bottle in my direction, and the guy looks over at me curiously for a moment, an assessing look on his wide, sideburned face. I stand still as a stone sculpture. He nods suddenly, and I nod back, and then Travis is returning to me.

"Who was that?" I ask, wrapping my fingers around the bottle, concentrating on the icy glass.

"Oh, that was the drummer in the band. They're going to play in a few minutes, and he asked if I wanted to get in on it."

"I didn't know you played."

"Yeah, a little bass."

"So, are you going to?"

"Nah. I said I was with you."

I smile up at him.

❧

We walk back into the small upstairs bedroom together. We join the circle. I breathe in the sharp scent of pot hanging low and hazy in the air. Someone has put on music, something whispery soft and repetitive.

"Just in time," the guy I think is James says, and passes a brass pipe to Travis. I swallow hard, look at Lila, but Erica is braiding and unbraiding her hair slowly and Lila seems to be enjoying it while staring dreamily at the ceiling.

Then it is my turn and I take the pipe, fit my mouth around the warm stem, and breathe in a fraction. "You can take a little more," James says. "It won't bite you." For some reason, this makes everyone laugh, and so I inhale again, and a biting sensation is exactly what I do feel flooding the back of my throat and the hollows of my eardrums. I swallow, hand the pipe off, swallow again, a bitter taste in my mouth. I wait for something to happen.

"It's cool if you've never smoked before," Travis is saying earnestly, and I nod. Then I feel like I am nodding too much and stop. "So, like, what kinds of stuff did you do in California?"

"The usual kinds of stuff. Movies, the beach." I wonder if this counts as him asking about me, and I lean forward, but by now the pipe has arrived again. Travis closes his eyes, takes a deep hit, pins his mouth closed. It seems like forever until his throat ripples a little and he exhales a thin stream of white smoke.

I try again. This time the burning sensation blurs over, and I, too, hold the smoke in my mouth until I feel like I am underwater, needing to surface. I exhale.

"Is it done yet?" the girl next to me says, and together we peer at the dry, dusty bits lining the bowl of the pipe. This strikes me as infinitely amusing, and I start giggling, managing to stop only when I notice Erica staring at me.

"You're so stoned," she pronounces, but her words are slurred, and she slumps sideways, her head falling into Lila's lap. I look for Lila to wink at me or make some sort of face, but Lila is leaning with her head back against the wall, her eyes closed.

"Load it up again," the girl next to me complains, her voice drawing out into a thin whine. James extracts a small plastic bag from the pocket of his cargo pants and meticulously begins packing the pipe again.

Someone gets up, people change places, and then the music changes, too, becoming something more pulsing and insistent.

"Where'd you get this stuff?" Travis asks after a while. "It's hard core."

"Kind bud. Only the best for you, man, only the best," James answers.

Someone is giggling softly, and I bite down hard on my lip to make sure it's not me. The music is beginning to throb, and the room shrinks steadily, the outlines of the furniture menacing.

"I think I can feel all the particles of blood rushing through my veins," I say to Travis, and hc nods slowly.

"That must be a pretty weird feeling," he offers, and I feel myself give a slow, hazy smile up at him, so grateful that he understands.

"I have to get out of here," I add, but Travis only looks blankly at me, and I realize that I may not have actually uttered the words.

Everyone either has their eyes closed or has fallen sideways like Erica and the girl next to me. Except for Ollie. He is sitting in the open window waving at me. I get up and walk over to him.

"Want to come outside?" he asks when I put my hands on the sill.

I breathe in cool air, imagining it as a light green mist billowing into my lungs.

"Not that way," Ollie adds hastily when I lean out even farther. "I'll meet you downstairs, okay?"

I look behind me. Travis is lying on the floor, his fingers drumming slowly on his chest, but Lila's eyes are open now, and she is watching me. I make a motion toward the door, slide through it before she can respond.

❧

I stumble down the deck stairs, push my way past a knot of people who all seem to be talking at once.

Then I am scrambling over the low stone wall, following the distant hollow boom of the waves as they pound into sand. The beach is empty in the moonlight. I slip off my shoes and wander down a few feet to let the water spill over my toes. When the waves recede, a piece of seaweed is clinging to my ankle. I bend over and all the blood bursts in a silvery rush of sound at my temples.

"Sadie," Ollie says suddenly, and I straighten up. My brother is standing a few feet away. He turns, walks toward the slice of moon hanging in the sky. I follow, fitting each of my footprints into his.

"My feet are bigger than yours now," I complain, leaning down to study the outlines of our combined tracks. A wave slaps into my face and I nearly tip over in surprise. Dabbling my hands in the water, I try to catch the pieces of reflected moon.

"Ollie, Ollie, Ollie, home free," I murmur–the charm, the childhood chant we used to cry whenever we touched home base. Safe.

❧

"There you are, Caldwell," Lila says, comes to sit beside me on the low stone wall. A light rain has started to fall, enough to drive most everyone back inside. "Where'd you go?"

"Just for a walk." I rub the raindrops from my bare arms, a Sisyphean task.

"By yourself?"

I hesitate. "Yeah." I shift, feeling the smooth stone under my thighs. It is cold here in the sea wind, but I don't want to say this and have Lila suggest we go back inside. I turn, study her profile.

"You'd make a good sculpture," I tell her. She looks at me, surprised. Then a sudden thought strikes me. "Hey, Lila, if Erica is a poodle, what kind of animals do you think we'd be?"

I can tell Lila is intrigued by the question because she puts one finger on her chin, falling into what she likes to call her "thoughtful pose."

"I think you'd be a cat," I decide. "A little black cat. Maybe a kitten, because you like to bat things around."

She giggles, gives me a shove. "What things do I bat around?"

"Oh, you know. Cats are mercurial. One minute, they're sleeping, the next they're stalking something."

"Okay. I'll take that. And you would be . . . let me think," Lila says, and she looks at me so intensely that I close my eyes. "I think a horse."

"Thanks a lot!"

"Shut up, I mean it. Horses are beautiful. Okay, a colt. All shy and long-legged and–"

"Clumsy? Hay-eating?"

"No! Sweet."

I lean my head on her shoulder. My brother would have been a colt, too, I think.

Chapter Fifteen ❧

On Sunday, after the party, I ride my bike to Lila's. I announce this intention at breakfast, and my mother looks up from stirring what seems like a pound of maple sugar into her oatmeal. "That's too far. All the way on the other side of town. We can give you a ride," she offers quietly. I look over toward the end of the table. The newspaper that has swallowed up all sight of my father trembles slightly.

"No. I want to ride my bike. It'll be fun."

My mother abandons all pretense of eating and picks up her mug of tea instead. She blows on it several times, says finally, "Call us when you get there?" Her voice is so hopeful, I can't refuse.

"I will."

My father folds down a corner of his newspaper and smiles at me.

❧

My front tire crunches over the gravel of Lila's driveway. I jab at the kickstand with my foot a few times before it reluctantly drops down and anchors the bike. I am suddenly, bitingly self-conscious. Lila had mentioned that I could drop over anytime, but I wonder what she will think about my bike.

Yet all Lila says when she answers the door and leads me into the kitchen is, "Nice wheels."

"Thanks," I say nonchalantly, looking around. Every surface

seems to be full of clutter. Keys, books, papers, stuffed animals, two bottles, three teething toys, and half of what looks like pieces of a mobile are all spread out on the kitchen table. Two gallon-sized scraped-clean jars of peanut butter and a Smucker's grape-jelly jar are crowded up against the side of the sink, next to a mess of dishes globbed over with jam dabs and toast crusts.

There is an extremely loud thump overhead, followed by two smaller ones, and then someone begins wailing. "Oh, God," Lila says in her most dry and calm voice. "Be right back." She saunters out of the kitchen, her flip-flops slapping at the floor.

I wander over to the wall near the refrigerator, hopping over a sticky pile of ooze that seems to be seeping out from under the oven, to study what looks like a series of family portraits. There are several shots of Lila surrounded by three brown-haired little boys. The boys are always grinning, and someone or other always seems to be missing a tooth. In what looks like the latest picture, Lila, wearing a red turtleneck, holds a small baby on her lap, who is stuffing a chunk of her hair into his mouth.

Lila's eyes are fixed somewhere beyond the scene, as if she just happened to wander into the picture and decided to sit and pose. I am reminded of those early medieval paintings of the Virgin Mary, the flat, calm expression she always wore.

"Oh, hello," says a startled voice, and I jerk backward with surprise. A woman is standing in the kitchen doorway, holding the same baby from the photo on one hip. Pieces of her hair straggle down from the knot high on her head. Her lips are dry and cracked, traces of her lipstick seem to have fled to the corners of her mouth. "I didn't know we had company," she says, and her voice deepens exactly the way Lila's does when our teacher asks her to read aloud in class.

I smile, hold out my hand. The baby gives a weak slap at it.

"No, sweetpea, no, no," the woman croons, jiggling the baby

a little. He offers me a toothy, drooling grin, flaps his arms. "I'm Lila's mother, Mrs. Harris," she says finally, shifting and holding out her hand. Two rubber bands circle her wrist. They look like they are cutting into her pale skin. I take her hand, shake it, look her directly in the eye the way my father always taught us to.

"I'm Sadie, Lila's friend from school."

"Oh?" She suddenly smiles at me, and the three lines carved into her forehead spring upward. "You're the one who helps her in English?"

I shrug. "Just the poems part. I really like those. Now we're onto plays. She's much better at those than I am–"

"Well, you're doing a wonderful job," Mrs. Harris says almost over me. "I'm so glad she found someone who actually thinks school is worthwhile."

"Oh, um, yeah. Yes." I nod reverently.

Mrs. Harris wanders over to the counter, picks up a crumbled piece of crust from one of the plates, holds it out to the baby. He contemplates the offering for a few seconds, eyebrows jutting together in a surprisingly adult expression, before he takes it and jams it into his mouth. She sets him down in the playpen, pulls open a drawer, and fishes out a large ball of rubber bands. She snaps the two from her wrist, works them expertly around the mass, ignoring the baby's clutching fingers. Then she slips the ball back into the drawer and returns to the sink. Flipping on the faucets, she drizzles cloudy yellowish liquid from an almost empty oversized plastic bottle onto the pile of dishes.

There is another crash overhead, but I seem to be the only one who notices. The baby is now happily cramming a tiny gray stuffed elephant through a rip in one side of the playpen netting, and Mrs. Harris is attacking the dishes.

"So," she says over the steam filling up the sink. I wonder

that she doesn't seem to feel the heat of the water, which she is repeatedly plunging her hands into. "Lila mentioned that you moved from Africa."

I blink. "California, actually–"

"I could have sworn she said Africa," Mrs. Harris interrupts, and her voice is a little more strident. She doesn't seem to be intending to use the dishwasher, and peering through the half-open door, I see why. It is filled with toys and several pairs of shoes caked in mud. "Connor, stop doing that," she says sharply. The baby ignores her, intent on working the whole toy through the opening. He gives a little cawing noise of triumph, then a wail as his elephant falls to the floor out of reach of his outstretched fat fingers.

I look at Mrs. Harris for a clue, but she is staring into the sink, grinding her lower lip between her teeth, elbows working furiously as dishes are thoroughly scraped, scrubbed, rinsed. I have a sudden vision of what bath time must be like. After a minute, during which Connor cries in broken little gulps, I lean over and offer him the toy. He stares at me for a minute, so I drop the toy in the playpen next to his foot. He resumes crying.

"Ignore him," Mrs. Harris says. "That's why I was a little startled when I saw you. I thought you would have been black. Now why did Lila say that?" She stares down at her reddened palms as if looking for the answer.

I look back at the baby, poke my tongue out the side of my mouth three times fast. He stops crying abruptly, gives me an astonished look, then bursts into fresh tears.

Mrs. Harris brushes past me, scoops Connor out of the playpen, jiggles him until he stops sniffling.

"Ready to go?" Lila says from the doorway. She has changed her outfit and is now wearing different jeans, the ones that flare into wide bells, and the pink T-shirt that sets off her black hair. Her lip gloss is freshly shining, and her cheeks are glowing. I feel grubby just standing next to her. "Mater," she says as she passes by, pinches Connor's nose lightly. He grins and holds out his arms for her, but she ignores him.

"Where are you girls off to?" Mrs. Harris asks, and her voice has sharpened again. "I really could use some help later, Lila."

"Of course," Lila says, her voice empty. "We're just going to the beach for a few hours."

"Dressed like that?"

"Like what?" Lila says, and now her voice has that dangerously soft quality that she uses with Erica sometimes. But her mother doesn't seem to notice.

"I need you to watch Connor later today while I take Billy and Simon to the–"

"Okay, Mom. Can I go now?"

"Fine," Mrs. Harris says. "But take the soda cans with you. You can return them to the center." She opens the cabinet under the sink, pulls out two shopping bags overflowing with empty Diet Coke and Sprite cans. "And with the money, I want you to pick up a gallon of milk and a box of macaroni, okay?" But her "okay" doesn't seem like a question, and Lila doesn't answer, just takes the bags by the handles and walks out the door.

I smile at Mrs. Harris, say weakly, "Thanks."

"Sure," she says blankly, and I scoot after Lila. Behind me, I can hear Connor start to cry again.

❧

We drive to the beach mostly in silence, the wind leaking through the cracks in the floorboard of the car. Although she wears her customary bored expression, Lila's hands seem too tight on the wheel. When we're at the turn-off for the beach road, I venture, "So, your mom seems nice."

At first I think she won't answer, but then she says, "Can you believe she once wanted to be an actress?"

"Like you?"

"Yeah."

"And what happened?"

"Nothing," she shrugs. "And then, me."

"Oh," I say. "Well, does she know *you* want to be an actress?"

Lila gives me a dark look. "Oh, she knows. She pretends not to hear me when I tell her I'm not going to college. But she knows."

Lila parks in a shady spot a few yards away from the stone steps that lead down to the beach. I draw in a deep breath of air that smells like salt. The color jumbling inside my head is an anxious orange. As if she can see this, Lila puts her hand over my wrist, a quick touch of fingers. "Relax. Stick shift is hard. But you'll get it."

We switch places, and I adjust the rearview mirror, gaze at the empty backseat. Then I look forward, past the spider-web crack in the windshield.

Ollie's skinny legs flash into view as he scrambles over the hood of the car. I squeeze my eyes shut. When I open them again, far out over the ocean, a white blur of a seagull dips into a dive. It plummets, pulls up at the last minute, skims the surface of greenish gray water.

❧

I insist on helping Lila at the recycling center, even though she tries to make me wait in the car. Under harsh fluorescent light, we feed the cans into a round hole in a giant hulking box of a machine. I listen to the sucking and crushing sounds of mangled aluminum. When the last can is gone, the machine rumbles, spits out clinking change for a long moment into Lila's cupped hands. "I like to pretend I'm at the slot machines in Vegas," she murmurs, and I laugh. Then I notice she isn't even smiling.

She does make me wait in the car when we get to the grocery store. "It's no big deal, Caldwell. I'll run in and run out." And before I can answer, she strides away, her purse jangling with the weight of the coins.

Twilight is blanketing the parking lot of the store and the overhead pole lamps flip on with a mechanical buzz, splotching the pavement with weak light. I watch several shoppers enter and exit the neon hub of the grocery store, before I release my seat belt, climb awkwardly into the driver's seat. I crank the window all the way down, let my arm hang out. Then I put my hands on the wheel, swallow, try to get used to the totally bizarre feeling of being alone in a car. I close my eyes, try to conjure up the rushing sound of the road beneath the wheels, the feel of wind–

"Usually people keep their eyes open while driving."

I scream. Ryan is standing at the driver's-side window, and for one irrational second, I expect to see his father looming behind him. I can't help the quick surreptitious scan for a police car. "You're alone?" I ask at last.

He looks confused by the question. "Yes," he says, as if this should be obvious. "I usually am. Why?"

I shake my head. "Did you have to sneak up on me like that? What are you doing, anyway?"

"Walking home." He swings his briefcase toward the far edge of the parking lot, which is hemmed in by a tall metal fence. In the deepening shadows, I notice a large gaping hole near the bottom half. "Shortcut. What are you doing?"

"Just . . . nothing." I push at the door and Ryan steps back so I can climb out of the car. We stand next to each other by the hood of the Beetle. He is wearing a gray sweatshirt that says TASTY AND GOOD FOR YOU. "How come I haven't seen you in school for a while?"

He smiles sweetly at me. "Did you miss me that much?"

"As if." A woman is pushing a shopping cart across the pavement, one wheel clattering out of tune with the other three. "Seriously, where have you been?"

"Suspended." He sets his briefcase between his legs. "You know, *suspended* means to debar someone briefly from privilege or office. But another meaning is, to be kept from sinking or falling. So, one version sounds pretty dire, but the other"–he lifts his shoulders, lets them fall–"not so bad." Then he shoves his hands in his pockets. "Sorry. I've had some time to think about the word. I had to write an essay on the meaning of it all." His voice takes on a lecturing tone, and I wonder whom he is imitating. But I ask the easier question.

"What'd you do?"

"Spread a little truth to the masses. It didn't go over big."

"It doesn't usually."

Ryan looks at me, and I can't tell if it is admiration on his face or something else. "So, what's in the briefcase?" I ask, feeling greatly daring.

"Passports, tickets to a foreign land."

"No, really."

He looks right and left with an overly mysterious air, crouches, checks under the car until I laugh. Then he sits back on his heels, dials the combination, and the locks open with a soft *snick*. I crane my neck, try to make out the titles of what seems like a dozen or so books. *Gunga Din, 1984, Hitchhiker's Guide to the Galaxy, The Once and Future King, Sorrow of Empires, The*

Fellowship of the Ring. I swallow. Ollie had never gotten to finish that one.

"You like fantasy?" I say now, through the sudden cold press of grief in my throat.

"Well, this planet isn't turning out that hot." His voice is flippant.

"You ever feel like you're losing a part of yourself?" I ask, hoping desperately that he will understand what I mean. He looks up from restacking his books, and I don't turn away as he studies my face. Behind his glasses, his eyes seem very dark.

"What's wrong, Sadie?" he asks quietly.

But before I can answer, I see Lila making her way toward us, a white gleam of a shopping bag in one hand. "Um . . . nothing. Forget it." I step back a little, my hip grazing the driver's-side mirror.

Ryan looks over his shoulder. The locks on his briefcase sound like gunshots as he snaps them closed. He straightens up. "Good luck with the losing-yourself part," he murmurs, and before I can answer, he walks away.

Lila approaches the car, maneuvers the plastic shopping bag sagging under the weight of the milk jug into the backseat. She is silent as we both climb back into the car, silent as she starts the car and rolls up the window that I had opened earlier. After one quick assessment of her impassive face, I keep my gaze trained resolutely forward as we sweep out of the parking lot.

"The whole fucking grocery line looked at me like I was dirt when I had to count out all that change to pay for the milk," she says finally, her voice low and bitter.

I turn to her, but before I can say anything at all, she adds, very softly, "Be careful, Sadie."

CHAPTER SIXTEEN

On Monday morning, I push open the glass doors of the school's main office. I come to a stop at Mrs. Clemont's desk and fumble in my backpack for the permission slip.

I don't want to look at the signature that Lila so carelessly, so easily, scrawled, looping her *l*'s so extravagantly. I had gone through my mother's papers, found a bank statement with a returned check, and had brought it to Lila in the Student Center earlier that morning. All around us, the hum and crush of preclass noise reverberated in my ears, but I kept my eyes focused on the permission slip, on Lila's hand hovering over the blank line. She studied the check in her left hand, made a few swirling motions in the air with her pen, then without a second's hesitation, she wrote an almost exact replica of my mother's signature.

"There," she said, holding up the paper. She pursed her lips, blew a breath onto the page, and the edges of the paper flapped lightly. "Not bad," she said, and handed it to me.

"It's amazing," I said, staring down at my mother's writing.

"What can I say? I'm gifted like that."

Now I stand, shifting from foot to foot, before Mrs. Clemont's desk as she makes soothing noises to someone on the phone. I feel unsteady on my feet, as if I am standing in sand. Trying to appear calm, bored even, I look through Mr. Anderson's door, which is slightly ajar.

The principal is leaning across his shiny walnut-colored desk, talking to someone I can't see. He keeps jabbing his forefinger down on his desk blotter, as if emphasizing whatever he is saying, and I shift closer, trying to listen.

"Do you really want that?" Mr. Anderson is asking earnestly, but he is either getting no answer or not getting the right answer, because he repeats the question. "You've already been suspended once this year. Don't you want to fit in?" he asks finally, an edge of irritation in his voice.

"Not really." I know that voice, and I can't help edging a little closer to the door.

"Why not?" Mr. Anderson says, and now there is no mistaking his annoyance. I sigh. I feel a little bad for Mr. Anderson. Whenever he sees me in the hall, he smiles his wide smile, asks how I am doing. I know he has no idea what my name is, but still, it's nice.

"I'm not interested in conforming. Sir." The last word is uttered so politely, so sincerely, so carefully designed to insult.

"So you don't want to fit in? Have friends? Have a normal high school experience?"

"What's normal, sir?" the person asks, and I bite my lip.

"Ryan," Mr. Anderson begins, and now he sounds tired. "You're an intelligent boy, you–"

"Oh, I know that," Ryan interrupts, his voice sure and even. "That's the whole problem with me, isn't it? That I don't want to fall into the factory line to be processed and packaged like the rest of those cretins out there. That I refuse to be defined and labeled and put on a shelf. That I don't want to grow up to be a model citizen content to let Big Brother tell me what to do and what to think and how to feel. So I won't get to fit in," he says, and now his voice is coated with a cheerful, almost friendly, sarcasm. "So I won't have the normal high school experience. So I won't get to pull out my Pioneer yearbook ten, fifteen years from now and show my beautiful blond wife and my 2.4 beautiful

blond, blue-eyed children all the wonderful scenes and snapshots from my wonderful high school experience. Oh, well."

I don't want to look at Mr. Anderson, don't want to see the crown of his shiny bald head dip downward in defeat.

"Sadie," Mrs. Clemont says, and I jerk my eyes back to her face. She is off the phone, and I think she has been for some while. Now she exchanges a glance with me, rolls her eyes toward the door. "Some people are determined to complicate their lives unnecessarily." Her tone is smug, complacent.

I thrust the paper toward her, and the three twenty-dollar bills that I have folded over and over until they are small, tight green packets. "I want to take Driver's Ed."

"Fine. That's fine," she says, scanning the paper. I expect her eyes to widen, her eyebrows to jump dramatically toward her forehead. I expect she will ask me to wait right here while she makes a telephone call or speaks to the principal.

"Wait right here," she says, her tone purposeful. She bustles up and away from her desk, her skirt making a swishing sound.

Tiny pearls of sweat form along my hairline. I knew this would never work. In the Student Center, Lila had seemed so sure. Now I wish I had asked her to come with me. Somehow, her presence would have offset all this. Mrs. Clemont wouldn't have been suspicious. Now she is going to call my mother. My mother who will turn pale and shake and go lie down on her bed and probably never get up again after she finds out what I've done, after she learns that I betrayed her by wanting to learn–

"Here you are," Mrs. Clemont says, turning back around. She is holding out a blindingly yellow textbook. I glance down at the cover. A boy, wearing a pastel blue shirt with a large collar, is sitting behind the wheel of a red car. He grips the wheel with both hands, his face wearing a look of calm determination. "Try

not to mark it up," she advises. "We do collect them back at the end of the class."

"Thanks," I manage to say, my voice sounding staticky. I clear my throat. "Thanks," I say again.

She nods. "Oh, wait, let me mark down the serial number of the book."

I surrender it back into her hands, peer through Mr. Anderson's open door again. He is making swift writing motions on a yellow pad of paper, his pen moving decisively across the page. Finally, he stands up, and Ryan must have come to his feet also, because now he is in view. He offers his hand across the desk, and after a moment, Mr. Anderson extends his arm. They shake hands politely, like two strangers being introduced for the first time. "Stay out of trouble, now," Mr. Anderson warns.

"Keep up the good work, Andy," Ryan replies, and steps through the opening of the doorway. He is swinging his briefcase in one hand.

"Mrs. Clemont," he says. "Always a pleasure to see you." Then he notices me. "Hey, again." I am startled by the genuinely happy note in his voice, especially after yesterday. He is wearing a yellow T-shirt that says I'M NOT RAPPAPORT in large black letters.

"Hi," I say belatedly. "How are you?"

"Sadie," Mrs. Clemont says sharply behind me. Flustered, I turn, accept the book from her once more. Her lips have flattened into tight, thin lines, and I kneel down awkwardly by her desk, try to stuff my book into my already overflowing backpack. The door to the office whispers open, shut.

"Well, that went well," Mr. Anderson's voice says from somewhere above me. "I don't want to call in his parents. Not after that last suspension. You get the sense that wouldn't help.

But I don't know what to do with that kid. Last week, Judy asked that he be removed from her French class because she got tired of having to answer questions on why the French didn't resist–"

"Hmmmm." Mrs. Clemont cuts across whatever Mr. Anderson was about to say.

I stand, flushed, swing my bag up and onto my shoulders.

"Hello there, young lady," Mr. Anderson says, and his face creases into a generous smile. I smile back.

"Hi, Mr. Anderson," I say, my voice soft.

"Sadie," Mrs. Clemont emphasizes brightly, "just signed up for Driver's Ed."

I swallow, suddenly reminded of my crime. I must look nervous, because Mr. Anderson gives a chuckle, the kind adults give when they are trying to sound like they know exactly where you're coming from. "Nothing to it, Sadie," he says. "You'll be fine. Of course, take it seriously. A lot of accidents happen because people didn't pay attention when they were driving." His eyebrows jam upward. "Don't look so worried, Sadie, you'll be–"

"I have to go," I whisper, and run. Outside the office, I lean against the wall, put my hand to the dog tag around my neck, pull the chain until it almost cuts into my skin.

Chapter Seventeen

"Well?" Lila says when I pull out the chair beside her. She sets down her copy of *The Merchant of Venice*, waits with a patient expression on her face as I ease my backpack off my shoulder and rub at my skin where the strap has chafed it. I pull out a bag of pretzels and set them on the table, examine the poetry wall, as I've come to call it. Not even the faintest outlines of last week's inspiring message remain, but I remember the words.

IF YOU CAN MAKE ONE HEAP OF ALL YOUR WINNINGS
AND RISK IT ON ONE TURN OF PITCH-AND-TOSS

"No problem," I say, grinning at her.

She grins back. "Told you." She rips open the bag, helps herself to a pretzel stick, bites into it. "Mmmm, honey mustard. My favorite." She chews thoughtfully. "See? You were freaking out for nothing."

"Freaking out about what?" Erica asks, coming to land at the table. She sets down two notebooks and rests her tiny glittery-pink iPod on top of them.

"Sadie's taking Driver's Ed," Lila says.

Erica looks at me, says incredulously, "You can't drive yet? Aren't you, like, seventeen already?"

"I'm sixteen," I say, trying to keep my voice mild.

"Did you skip a grade?" she asks finally.

"That would be the logical conclusion," Lila says from behind her book again.

But Erica seems focused on me, waiting for an answer. "Yeah," I reply. "I did."

"So you're, like, really smart," Erica concludes, the word *smart* falling off her tongue like an insult. She wrinkles up her nose like she has just walked behind a garbage truck. I stare at her.

"Here's a piece of earth-shattering news," Lila says, looking at Erica from the top of her book. "It's not the fifties anymore. Guys actually like girls who can read."

I look down at my hands, afraid I might laugh, afraid I might feel sorry for Erica, who must be wondering why it is that everything she says these days comes out wrong. When I look up, the moment has passed. Erica is plugged into her iPod and is nodding determinedly to whatever she is listening to. Her face is slightly flushed, but that is the only sign. Meanwhile, Lila is reading again, blithely crunching through my pretzels.

"I saw Fryin' Ryan in Mr. Anderson's office," I offer, but no one seems to want to take me up on this. Lila reaches for another pretzel, her eyes on her book. Three tables over, a girl is sitting in a guy's lap, their heads close together, and they begin kissing feverishly.

Mr. Hutchinson strolls over, politely taps the guy on the shoulder. The couple break apart, a dazed expression on their faces. Mr. Hutchinson spreads his hands to the heavens, as if saying, *Hey, it's not my rule, but.* The girl giggles, the guy scowls. As soon as Mr. Hutchinson walks away, they lean close to each other again, this time staring into each other's eyes.

"Disgusting, isn't it?" Lila murmurs besides me.

"Maybe they're so in love they can't help it," I point out. "Maybe they're like Romeo and Juliet," I add. We've just finished that play in English. Our teacher seems to be a Shakespeare fanatic.

"Carly and Tim?" Lila snorts. "They've been going out since third grade."

"I've heard he's cheating on her," Erica says. She has pulled the headphones from her ear, and now she winds the cord around one finger.

"I heard that, too," Lila says.

Encouraged, Erica leans forward. "With Kathy."

"Not surprised. She's a whore," Lila says, and I look at her. "What? She is."

"She's been taking money for blow jobs since we were twelve," Erica confirms for me.

I grimace.

"But I heard she did Tim for free," Erica adds.

"So, there's your Romeo and Juliet for you," Lila finishes, grins wide enough to include both Erica and me. Her eyes shift above my head. "Speaking of Romeos," she murmurs, and I grip the edge of the table with my fingers. "Be cool," she whispers as Travis drops into the seat beside me. I look at him, smile, look away. I notice Erica has straightened up in her chair and is now fiddling with her iPod again.

"What's up?" Travis says. This seems to be a general greeting for everyone, so I don't answer.

"Hi, Travis," Erica says, her voice all lit up.

He nods at her, then jerks his chair sideways.

"Do you want a pretzel?" I offer, and then think how childish, how stupid that sounds.

He shakes his head. "Listen," he begins in my general direction.

"Hey, Travis," Erica interrupts. "Have you heard that new song by Deranged Violets yet? I just downloaded it."

He looks at Erica vaguely, as if trying to connect the dots of what she is saying. "Yeah," he answers. "I did hear it. It's pretty good."

"I know, isn't it?" Erica answers, and there is a pride in her voice that irritates me. It's not like she wrote the stupid song. "What do you think of their–"

"I haven't heard that song," Lila interjects. She has set her book down again and is leaning forward. "Can I hear it, Erica?"

"Sure," Erica says, pushing her iPod across the table. She looks back at Travis.

"Do you–"

"But how do you work this?" Lila interrupts again.

"So, Sadie," Travis says to me. "Did you have fun at the party?"

"Yes," I say, wondering if I should be smiling more. "Your house is really cool." I jiggle my leg under the table. *He's talking to me, he's talking to me, me, me.*

"I don't have one, so these are kind of a mystery," Lila is continuing on my left. "How do I turn this on?"

"You just push this button here. No, not that one. No! Oh, give it to me!" Erica lunges across the table, pulls her iPod out of Lila's unresisting fingers. She frowns at the screen. "What did you do?"

"I don't know–"

"Sadie," Travis begins again. "Want to come outside for a cigarette with me?"

"Sure," I find myself saying. I throw one look at Lila, who winks at me. I follow Travis toward the double glass doors that lead to the outside.

The October air has a biting crispness to it, and I wrap my arms around myself, give a little hop. It is too early to wear the heavy down jacket that I picked out with my mother from a catalogue just last week, but I am wondering how much longer it will be. Travis and I look at each other, then away.

"Actually, I don't smoke," I say finally. Two sparrows that

have alighted on an apple core are busily arguing over it in tiny chirping fits and starts.

"Actually, I don't either," Travis says. He smiles, stuffs his hands into his pockets. "I just asked so we could come outside."

"Oh." I shiver a little, and in the next second, Travis is pulling off his jean jacket.

"Here," he offers, holding it out to me, and I take it, our fingers not meeting.

"Thanks," I say, and shrug myself into it. It is warm and smells good and clean and soapy. I try to draw in deep, but unnoticeable breaths. "I seem to always be cold."

"Well, I would imagine you would be. I mean, coming from California."

"True."

"So what about those pictures?" he asks.

"What? Oh. You really want to see some?" I try to figure out if he's teasing, but he looks serious.

"Sure. Maybe we could go out. Friday night. Dinner?"

I smile at him, a real smile. "That'd be very cool."

Chapter Eighteen ❧

My mother has been buying pumpkins, acorn squash, and gourds lately. Several pumpkins squat on the front doorstep, while two more guard the back door. The large copper platter on our mahogany dining room table is piled with mini pumpkins, and her blue cut-glass bowl is overflowing with round-bodied, long-necked gourds.

I don't know what her plans are regarding them, but I can only hope she doesn't want to cook them. I am in love with their lines and shapes and pebbled skin. Today, when I come home from school, I stop just long enough to grab my sketch pad and swipe some gourds off the kitchen counter before heading out to the beach, where the light is brightest. I have the shore mostly to myself, so I sit with my back against the stone wall, slip off my shoes, and draw.

I sketch them alone and in various combinations. I arrange them in pyramids. My fingers fly and fly and fly across the white pages, gourds blossoming under my fingers, the ocean waiting in the background.

I stop only when the light begins to fade. I set down my pad and pencils, close my eyes, and stretch, feeling something between my shoulder blades pop. Friday is four days away. I am four days away from improving my chances at being normal.

"Strange," a voice muses next to me. "I've never seen a mermaid with charcoal on her face."

My eyelids flutter open and Ryan swims into sight. He is looming over me, backlit by the setting sun, making me squint at him.

"You've never seen a mermaid," I answer. "And what did I say about sneaking up on people?" I rub charcoal-stained fingers on my jeans.

He sits down next to me, plunks his briefcase in the sand. It casts a long, narrow box of a shadow. "You have more on your face," he points out, but doesn't tell me where exactly and I don't ask. "And how do you know I've never seen a mermaid?"

I look at him. "Okay, Ryan, have you ever seen a mermaid?"

"No." He grins. "But that doesn't mean I'm going to give up trying. Just because we don't always see things, doesn't mean they aren't there."

I shiver a little, dig my toes into cold sand.

"What?" Ryan asks. His gaze is too intent on me.

"Nothing." I arrange my pencils into a neat row along the closed cover of my sketchbook. "Hey, which one of these houses is yours?" I indicate the long stretch of the beach and the houses, standing like sentinels. Ryan apparently finds this question funny, but he says only, "None."

"You don't live around here?"

He shakes his head. "I live on the"–he shapes his fingers into quotation marks–"wrong side of the tracks." He picks up one of my gourds, studies it, adds, "Which means a girl like you shouldn't be talking to a guy like me."

Unsure if this is a reference to Sunday, I veer into, "I saw you in Mr. Anderson's office today." My eyes are on the wash of clouds, now turning a dark goldy-pink.

"I know," Ryan says patiently. "I said hello to you, remember?"

I look at him for a moment, at his intelligent face, and wonder why he lets me get away with stupid moments like this, when his life seems to be a crusade against stupid people. "Are you getting suspended again? Is that why you were in Mr. Anderson's office?"

"Oh," Ryan says, stretching out the word like a rubber band. "Call it our weekly coffee chat. Minus the coffee." He pushes up his glasses with one finger. "He's worried about my prospects. Like my father, like my mother, whatever."

"And what are your prospects?"

"That, Sadie is a very good question. Something I hope I spend the rest of my life figuring out.

"Now it's my turn to ask the questions," he announces. "And I've got a really mundane one to start. What's up with you and Travis Hartshorn?"

"Nothing."

"Nothing? Rumor has it otherwise."

"What rumor?" I ask. "I hate that word, by the way."

"Ru-mor," Ryan says, drawing out the syllables. "Middle English? Old French? Latin," he decides, finally. "Moor, mooring. A piece of information with an uncertain, unstable mooring. I like to play with words." He tosses the gourd in the air, catches it. "Back to you and Travis Hartshorn."

I shrug. "I went to a party at his house the other weekend."

"Right. The annual bash."

"Let me guess, you've never gone."

"Never wanted to," he says, and I do believe him.

"It was okay."

"Did you get drunk?" He knocks his knee into mine. "Come on, you did."

"No."

He leans back, looks at me appraisingly. "I'm impressed."

"Why?"

"Because I thought that was the thing to do at these parties."

I cave to the pressure. "I did smoke a little pot."

"Oh, Sadie," Ryan says, and he sounds genuinely disapproving.

"What do you mean, 'oh, Sadie'?" I say, indignant. "You seem pretty antiestablishment."

"I am. But let's not get into that. And as for smoking pot, I have no problem with anyone else doing that. I'm all for legalizing it. Who cares if they kill off the ten brain cells they have left? You, on the other hand, are far, far too superior to be descending to their level. You actually have a brain. You are an artist, you are something different, the likes of which hasn't been seen before at Pioneer. You, I am convinced, just may be a mermaid in disguise."

I stare at him. At today's T-shirt, which reads ASK ME WHAT I KNOW. At his dark eyes, which shift like water. "*You* are too much," I say finally.

Ryan sighs. "Be that as it may, I expect more from you. Don't let me down, Sadie."

Chapter Nineteen ❧

"I have my first Driver's Ed class today," I remind Lila. "So don't call my house looking for me, remember?"

"Oh, yeah. I won't. I'll bc at rchcarsal anyway."

"Oh, that reminds me. Theater-geek boy came looking for you," Erica says. I look at her, confused, and she rolls her eyes. "Not you, Sadie. Not *everyone's* after you, you know."

"I never said they were," I answer softly.

"Ignore her," Lila whispers to me. She flips open the mustard-yellow covers of her Physics book, says in a louder voice, "Why aren't you in this class with me? Then I wouldn't have to study."

"Do you need help?" Erica puts in quickly. "We're not in the same class, but I think we've been over that chapter already."

Lila smiles beatifically at her. "Ah, Erica, the quality of mercy truly is not strained." She pushes her chair closer, frowns at the pages. "What does that even mean?"

"Let me get my notes," Erica says, dives into her bag.

Lila runs her finger down the page, then looks up at me as if she has just remembered something. "Oh, you can come by the theater afterward if you want a ride home. Maybe a little D.L.?"

I smile weakly at her code-speak. "Thanks, but this class is till, like, five thirty and . . ." My voice seems to stop working, and I pick up my can of Coke, drink several swallows, my lips tasting like aluminum.

"It'll be cool, Caldwell." Lila tilts her head to one side, as if to consider this some more. "Well, no," she amends, "it'll be boring as hell. But you'll survive."

❧

My hands feel damp and I scrub them awkwardly across my jeans as I hurry down what feels like the endless hallway. *Please Ollie, please Ollie, please Ollie, don't make this so hard for me*. I realize that I am speaking aloud when the girl in front of me, her glossy brown ponytail swinging with each step, throws a surprised look over her shoulder. She hitches her backpack higher, begins to walk faster, but I lengthen my stride, overtake her, making sure that I am humming audibly.

Finally, room 360 looms up on my left, and I duck into it. There are six guys scattered throughout the room, and not one of them is my brother. I remember how to breathe. Judging from the words *DRIVER'S ED* written in thick chalky letters on the blackboard, I am in the right place. The man sitting behind the teacher's desk looks up at me, smiles. His face is broad and red, the entire lower half covered in a thick brown beard.

"Welcome to Driver's Ed," he says. "You must be Sadie, right?" He stares at me. "And how do I know this?" he says solemnly, tapping his temple with one thick finger. "Am I psychic, you ask yourself? Nope! You're the only girl enrolled in class this time! That's how!" He begins to chuckle and seems to be so delighted with himself, that I offer him a nervous smile back. "First time that's happened in twelve years. Usually have a big mix. I'm Coach Vesecki, by the way," he adds, holding out his hand to shake. I take it. "Whoa, cold hands, Sadie." Then he winks at me. "Warm heart, right?"

I stare at him as he laughs broadly. It seems he will continue to laugh until I make some sort of response, so I smile again. Weakly. Finally, he stops, wipes at his eyes, gestures at the desks. "Have a seat with the rest of these delinquents."

I choose a seat not too close to the front of the room, but not in the last few rows, either. The guy nearest me, wearing a red bandanna around his head, seems to be asleep with his eyes open. I take out my notebook, open it to a fresh blank page, pull out my pen.

"Prepared," Coach Vesecki comments approvingly. "She's *prepared.* The rest of you nitwits could learn a thing or two from this little lady here. Okay," Coach Vesecki continues, and all of a sudden, his voice is much louder, as if amped to fill a stadium and not just the tiny confines of room 360. He picks up a pointer that has been leaning against the wall next to the chalkboard. "Welcome to Driver's Ed. This is a six-week course where, if you pay attention, you will learn the fundamentals of driving. A car is your passport to freedom. It's the great American right besides life, liberty, and the pursuit of happiness. When you have a car, people look at you differently. You become someone to respect. When you have a car, women will give you guys a second look. Probably, after getting a second look at you guys, she won't give you a third, but hey"–Coach Vesecki spreads his hands and shrugs–"it's a start. A lot more than a lot of you guys have now. Am I right?"

I steal a look at the rest of the room. My neighbor still seems to be asleep, but a few of the guys appear slightly more interested.

"Let's appeal to the only woman present here. Sadie!" Coach Vesecki's voice booms out, and I jump. "Would you look at any of these losers . . . " He pauses, reconsiders. "Ah . . . young men here if they didn't have cars?"

"Um . . . well . . ."

"Exactly my point!" Now his voice deepens as he says, "A car is not just a toy, lady and gentlemen. A car is a weapon. A machine of death. And if you're not careful, you can become a killer. A killer, I said." He nods a few times, raps the pointer on the word *ED.* "Now, to start off, we're going to watch a fine film that all, uh . . . aspiring drivers should be required to see." He bends over the portable unit, and the TV springs to blue-screen life. The words *Death on the Highway* appear in bold black letters. Then they flash three times before the screen freezes.

I glance across at my neighbor, who is now awake and picking at his fingernails. Slowly, he tears a tiny strip of skin off his thumb. I swallow and focus on the word *HI* carved into my desk, running the tip of my ballpoint pen through the grooves of the letters. I don't want to see this video. I don't want to see accidents and mangled car parts and limbs strewn all over the highway or whatever else this movie is going to contain. I visualize myself picking up my backpack and fleeing.

The door swings open, and I look up to see Ryan ambling toward me. He swings his briefcase up onto the desk next to mine, slides into the chair. The silence in the room changes, becomes charged, as Coach Vesecki lowers caterpillar-thick eyebrows and glares at Ryan. "Think you'll make it through this time?"

"Probably not," Ryan answers cheerfully.

They seem to be locked in a stare-off until Coach Vesecki shakes his head. "Boy," he says, "Your father is the salt of the earth, and how the apple fell so far from the tree is beyond me."

"Uh, Coach," someone pipes up from the back of the room. "Don't you know that Fryin's father is really a mass murderer?"

Everyone laughs except for me, Coach Vesecki, and Ryan. The TV screen goes fuzzy with static.

"So what's a nice girl like you doing in a crummy joint like this?" Ryan says elaborately out of the side of his mouth. He unsnaps the locks of his briefcase.

"I didn't know you didn't have your license," I whisper.

"Actually, I've been driving since I was ten."

"Right."

"Boy Scout's honor," he says, holding up two fingers.

"You were never a Boy Scout!"

"I love your indignation, Sadie. It's one of your best qualities." He grins at me, unfolds a copy of the *New York Times* from his briefcase, and dives into it.

"What a loser," my neighbor says next to me, apparently awake again. He sucks at one finger, making a loud noise. Someone's cell phone rings, an insistent techno beat.

Coach Vesecki turns, all traces of good humor gone. "You know the school policy. No phones in class. Well?" he barks. A guy in the back corner sheepishly holds up his glowing phone. Coach Vesecki barely glances at him, stares disgustedly at Ryan's newspaper for another minute before turning back to the VCR.

"Is it broken, Coach?" one guy finally asks. "Should we go home?"

Coach Vesecki flaps a hand at us, picks up the remote control. "Naw. Hold on a minute here. Minor technical problems."

Ryan folds down one corner of his newspaper, whispers, "I can just imagine that's what he says to his wife every night."

❧

"How was it?" Lila asks me.

I shift the phone to my other ear, settle back on my bed. "It was okay. We watched–"

"Death on the Highway?"

"Yeah!"

"It's his favorite. He likes to show that one every semester."

"It's from, like, the eighties–the main guy, the one who drinks and drives, he had this mullet."

"It was probably really cutting-edge when Vesecki first started teaching. So, anyone interesting in your class?"

I pause. "Ryan. You know, Fryin' Ryan."

"Really?" Lila says, but I can tell she's not listening. "So, Erica said to me today–"

There is a clicking noise. "Hello?" I venture. "Hello?"

"I'm here," Lila says, now with a weary patience in her voice. "I'm on the phone."

There is silence, then, "Who are you taking to?" a childish voice asks.

"My friend. Get off the phone."

There is another silence.

"Billy, I can *hear* you breathing."

A loud jarring click. Lila sighs. "Anyway, Erica was asking if we could hang out at the mall tonight."

"Oh, yeah?"

"And I really don't want to unless you come."

"Really?" I try not to sound too pleased.

"It's colossally boring, hanging out at the mall, but you know Erica, she likes to be seen. So are you in?"

"Well, when you make it sound *that* appealing, sure."

"Good, so–"

There is another loud click and a burst of giggling.

"Billy!" Lila snaps.

"It's not Billy, it's Simon," says someone sounding exactly like Billy.

"Who cares who you are, just–"

"Mom says she needs you. You have to get off the phone." This is said in a singsong tone.

"Fine, I'll get off, but you better run." The phone clicks abruptly again and Lila sighs for the second time, the sound like rushing wind in my ear. "I have to go. I envy you being the only child." There is a pause. "I mean, now that you are."

I swallow.

"Sorry, Sadie," Lila says, and her voice is suddenly hesitant.

"It's cool," I say. "I'll see you later?"

❧

I am sitting in my seat before English class starts, drawing my fifth mermaid of the morning, when Lila comes in, her face more animated than usual. "Hey," she greets me. There is an undertow of excitement in her usually languid voice.

"What?" I ask.

"What, *what?*" she answers. I wait. She relents. "Okay, can you come over to my house on Sunday? For all day?"

"Probably. Why?"

"Maybe we shouldn't meet at my house," she muses. "Maybe the library instead. Yeah, that'll make it more legit."

"What are you talking about?"

She leans forward, presses her hands together as if to contain something from spilling over. "There's an audition in New York City. I really, really want to go. It's for this movie, with this new director who was featured last month in *Variety*. The projects he does are so amazing. Anyway, he doesn't have a huge budget or anything, so he can't go and hire anyone really famous, and maybe, just maybe–"

"He'll look at you and think, '*Wow*, I've got to have this girl in my movie'?" I finish in a rush, giving a little jump sideways. "That's fantastic, Lila. Can I be your date for the Oscars?"

"Shhh," she reproves. "Don't jinx it. Probably nothing will happen, okay? But I have to try. So anyway, the call's in the city on Sunday at two. We can take the train in. What do you think?"

I nod. "Are you telling your mom?"

She shakes her head. "You?"

"No!" I hold out my hand and we shake, seal the deal.

"Good morning, class," Snore says, walking into the room. There is a collective shuffling-forward movement. Snore gazes out at all of us dispassionately for a moment, as he does every morning. I always shift and drop my eyes, but I've noticed Lila can hold his stare without blinking.

Now he holds up his copy of *The Merchant of Venice*, giving us a meaningful look, until everyone digs out his or her own copy and flicks pages in a busy-sounding way. "Page two-twenty-three, act four. Shylock's trial. The tragic moment of this play. Who shall read Shylock?" He considers the room, his gaze now thoughtful. "Mr. Stillman."

Mark Stillman scratches the back of his neck, takes off his baseball cap for a minute, then sets it back on his head.

"And please, Mr. Stillman, try not to butcher the English language this time." A faint titter sweeps the room, and now the back of Mark's neck is flushing lightly, but he grins anyway.

"And Portia," Snore continues, and he doesn't need to deliberate at all. "Miss Harris, if you will do the honors."

Lila nods, a queen accepting her due.

"Start with 'the quality of mercy,'" Mr. Snore says as he leans back in his chair, his eyes focused on the ceiling.

"'The quality of mercy is not strained,'" Lila begins, each word round and perfect, like jewels dropping from her tongue. Her voice is more passionate than I have ever heard, deeper and softer and fuller all at once. I glance at our teacher. His eyes are closed and a smile plays across his lips. I look at Lila and understand that she is gone from this room.

I pick up my pencil and begin to draw again, letting her words fall like rain.

❧

Friday night, every piece of clothing I own is on the floor, and I am sitting on my bed in my bathrobe, contemplating tears. Everything looks awful on me, too tight, too faded, too . . . not right. I search out the phone, buried under a blanket and my pillow. I scoop up my battered teddy bear that I've had forever, hug him to my chest, press the numbers with too much force.

"Help," I say when Lila answers on the third ring.

"Okay. Take a deep breath."

I take a breath.

"That didn't sound deep enough," she says accusingly, and waits until I blow out a noisy gust. "Seriously, what's wrong?"

"Clothes emergency."

"Wear your flowered jeans. Those are cool."

"And what top?"

"Any tank top will do."

"It's forty-five degrees out."

"Do you want to look good?"

"Yes." I kick at my dresser.

"Pink," Lila says decisively after a second. "You look good in pink. Pink is your color."

"Pink is *your* color."

"Pink is not my color."

"Everything is your color."

"I knew I liked you for a reason. Call me when it's over. Have fun walking the plank." She gives a dramatic cackle and clicks off.

❧

By 7:15, I am considering throwing up. I am sitting on my bed in my flowered jeans and a sleeveless rose-colored shirt. I sewed sequins onto the edges of the armholes at the last minute, more to conceal a tiny grape-juice stain than anything else. I don't need any blush because my cheeks look like someone slapped me hard. Twice on each side. But I do brush on a little more mascara. Then I get the undeniable impression that my eyelashes look like insect legs, clumpy and stiff, so I rub frantically at them, giving the skin under my eyes a smudged and bruised look. Then I have to spend three minutes and several Q-tips repairing the damage. I trace the outlines of the dog-tag necklace that I've hidden under my shirt. The metal is warm against my skin.

The doorbell rings, and I catapult off my bed. I take the stairs three at a time, miss the last step, land hard on my right ankle, wince, keep going. I swing around the banister and into the foyer, two steps ahead of my mother as she makes her way from the living room. I burst past her astonished face, have a dim impression of my father rising from his easy chair. "I *got* it," I insist, and brake at the front door. I take a breath. Then I pull the door open, extra slowly.

Travis is standing on my doorstep, his hands stuffed into his pockets, and I am alternately relieved and disappointed that there seem to be no flowers. But he is smiling at me, and I am smiling back, even though a tiny part of me thinks I am smiling too much.

"Hi," I breathe.

"Hi," he says back. "Ready?"

"Yeah, I–"

"Sadie," my mother calls behind me, in her best company voice, like light on glass.

❧

"So," my father says heartily. I cringe inwardly, feeling the word bouncing around the too-small space of the living room, where my parents have managed to corral us. "Sadie mentions you play football. How's the team doing this year, Travis?" My parents are both wearing tight-lipped, anxious grins, and I have to look away briefly, through the sliding glass doors into the cool and welcoming darkness of the side yard.

"Not too bad. We lost against Coe. And against Ramson High." Then Travis shrugs. "Our team usually loses," he says, almost apologetically, to my father.

My father nods in an understanding manner, touches the beak of the wooden duck resting on the mantelpiece, as if to stop it from swimming off into the air. "You'll get there," he says reassuringly, and I want to scream.

"Where are you two off to?" my mother asks somewhat abruptly.

"Um . . . dinner," I say, looking at the curve of blank space between my mother and father's heads, wishing I could throw myself into it.

Travis puts his hands in his pockets and smiles at the floor, a dimple appearing in his cheek.

"So, you shouldn't be home too–"

"Well, it was lovely to meet you," my father says, thrusting out his hand at Travis. They shake heartily for a minute. "Have fun, you two!"

"Thanks, Dad, Mom," I manage, and beeline for the door, not even checking to see if Travis is behind me.

❧

"That was fun," I say brightly. I click my seat belt into place, put my hands on my knees, my fingers tracing a flower patch.

"Your parents are nice," Travis says, his voice conciliatory. He backs out of the driveway, swift and sure. Too swift and sure. I know that my mother is watching behind the kitchen curtains and that she will probably be clocking the speed. "Your dad especially." He flips on his blinker. "He's not into football, is he?"

I shake my head. "Why?"

"He asked me if I played outfield or not."

I look at Travis for a minute, watch his dimple flicker once, twice, steady. We laugh.

"You're probably not into that stuff, either, huh?"

"Not really."

"Naw, you're an art chick. That's cool. I've never dated an art chick before."

I didn't know we were dating, but I do know enough to not point this out.

"But you should come to some more of the games. They're a lot of fun. Even if you're not into football."

I nod vigorously. "I went to one."

"Yeah." He smiles at me. "I know. And maybe," Travis offers as we smooth up to a red light. "Maybe we could go to . . . a museum or something."

"Yeah?" I can't help the delight in my voice.

"Yeah," he echoes. The DON'T WALK signal flashes pieces of orange light across the dashboard. "Can I just say how excellent you look tonight?"

I blink at him. "You can."

He bursts out laughing. "Okay. You look excellent. I like your hair."

Maybe I won't be sick after all.

❧

Travis holds open the frosted glass doors of the Country Squire Diner and I step in. I've already decided that I love the red booths and the waitresses in their pink-and-white checkered uniforms, with their tired faces and tight rolls of hair pinned to the tops of their heads. I love the old-fashioned jukebox in the corner and the multicolored glass lamps that hang from the ceiling. I think I would paint this all with a soft wash of yellow. I am loving everything–until a blare of sound swells and breaks over my ears.

"Yo, Hartshorn!"

I jerk my head over to where six guys are crowded in a booth. Glasses and cups and dirty plates cover every inch of the table in front of them. Six pairs of eyes are focused sharply on where we're standing. "Hartshorn . . . and a *lady*. Whoooeeeee!"

"Great," Travis says very softly from behind me, and as I twist to look back at him, he manages to smile, raise one hand. "Hey, guys," he calls, his voice suddenly deeper, carrying across the room. He brushes past me, makes his way over to the table.

There is a complicated round of hand slapping. I take a few steps toward the table, not knowing if I should just walk over and plant myself next to Travis's side or not. To my right, an old man is loudly slurping at a cup of soup, while a younger woman watches with an engraved air of weariness. As if feeling my eyes upon her, she glances up, so I stare at the menu rack.

"Sadie," Travis says. "C'mere." He beckons me over, not looking, and I make my way toward him. He puts an arm around my shoulders. "Don't be shy," he says, and I teeter off balance, press down hard with my heel, right myself. I have the uncomfortable feeling of being onstage before an audience of six very interested football players, but before I am required to say anything, a waitress, who looks only a few years older than me, bustles up to the table. "Hi, Travis," she giggles. "Do you want to sit with them?" she asks, picking up two oversized menus.

I look at Travis, offer no help. He shakes his head. "Naw. Not tonight."

I am trying to work out if there is any regret in his voice, when the waitress says, "Ooooh!" Her perfectly lined pink mouth puckers up. "Special date," she singsongs, leads us away. For one second, the table goes quiet, and then everyone erupts into whistles and cheers.

"Shut up," our waitress shrieks, as if they are calling to her. "They're animals," she murmurs to me, but she seems proud of them, even as she rolls her eyes exaggeratedly. She brings us to a booth that is thankfully on the other side of the restaurant. "I'll have to go calm them down."

I slide into the booth, study the menu in front of me. Finally, I look up, find Travis's eyes on me.

"Do you want to go somewhere else?"

Yes, please, thank you, God.

"No," I say. "Why would you ask?"

He shrugs. "I don't know. If you're uncomfortable with the guys being here."

"*I'm* not uncomfortable," I insist, my hand going reflexively to my throat. But from the way Travis fiddles with the menu, I don't know if he believes me.

"Hot date tonight!" one of the football players whoops. Our waitress is sitting in one of the football players' laps, giggling wildly.

"Let's go," Travis says, half rising.

"No!" I put out one hand, catch at his arm across the table. He locks his hand onto mine and sinks back down. "It's fine, it's fine, really." I risk a glance around, my eyes catching on the framed vintage magazine covers hanging on the walls. "I like this place a lot."

"Isn't it great?" Travis confesses. "And I thought since you're new in town, you'd want to see where we all hang out anyway, and . . ." He still seems worried, so I leave my hand in his.

"I'm glad." I wait a beat, add, "I brought some pictures." I still hadn't decided if he had been serious, so earlier in the day, I had selected only a dozen of my favorites and wound a rubber band around them.

"Of California? Let's see 'em."

I dig happily through my purse, pull out the packet.

"Um . . . those are a lot," Travis says, staring at the pile in my suddenly motionless hands. Then he looks up at me, laughs. "Just kidding, Sadie."

I nod, hesitate, then put the pile on the table. "So, this is a fig tree next to my house."

Travis nods, drumming his fingers on the table. "That's pretty cool."

"And this is the view from this really high mountaintop near me."

"And what's this?"

I crane my neck. "The desert. We went camping."

"Your friends?"

I shake my head. "No. My parents and me. It was this really amazing place. At night–"

"Yo, play that one I like. You *know* the one I like," Travis yells over my head, his voice suddenly deeper. An elderly woman dressed in a silk scarf and pearls, sitting alone at the table next to us, turns and stares at Travis. He doesn't seem to notice.

"Okay," he says, looks back at me, smiles. "So it was this cool camping place?"

I nod. "Yeah." I trace the outlines of the picture, press the tip of my finger into one corner, feeling the sharp point work into my skin.

"Do you like this song?" he asks after a minute.

I listen for a few beats. "Is it the Durangos?"

"That's right."

"Yeah, kind of."

"I have tickets to their show this December. Me and a bunch of people are going. You want to come? I could get you a ticket."

"That'd be–"

"Ohhhh," our waitress whispers, staring down at the tabletop. "It's picture time."

I am beginning to hate her.

"Do you know what you want?" Travis asks me, his menu still closed.

"A Coke. And the penne special," I say, dividing a look between him and the waitress.

She nods at me, her pen swirling across the page. "I *love* the penne. *Love* it." She nods up at the ceiling, and I wonder if she is thanking some god for the divine recipe. Then she beams at me, turns back to Travis. "She has good taste, Travis. You should really keep this one. If you can." She dings his elbow with her pen, and I decide that she's not so bad after all.

"Thanks, Anne. I'll take your advice to heart. Like I take all of your advice to heart. And I'll have the cheeseburger. Medium–"

"Yeah, yeah, yeah. Medium-well. Chocolate shake, right? Cheese fries? When are you going to branch out? Maybe *you* can help him with that." And before either of us answers, she skips off.

"Owner's daughter. She's like the older sister I never wanted." Travis wrinkles up his forehead in this extra-mournful way, and I decide to laugh. "So do you have any brothers or sisters?" he asks.

I shake my head, hastily avert my eyes from the counter stool on which Ollie is spinning and spinning. "Nope," I say.

"That's cool. So–"

There is a scuffle and stamping of feet as the football players begin standing up. One of them counts out a few singles, tosses them onto the table. He looks at Travis and me, comes over. "Yo, Hartshorn," he says, thudding to a stop at our table.

"Hey, Miller," Travis says equably enough.

"So what's the deal?"

"No deal."

"This why you couldn't hang out with us tonight?" Miller winks at me. "You're in my Chem class."

"Oh, yeah?" I say, even though I know this.

"Yeah. Maybe now you'll give me the time of day."

I stare at him.

"Miller thinks you're hot," Travis offers after a minute.

"Shut up," Miller says, puts Travis in a headlock. They punch at each other for a few minutes before some signal seems to occur to both of them and they suddenly release each other.

"I'm, like, failing that class," Miller continues.

I nod. "Yeah. Me too."

"Damn, and I was thinking you could tutor me and all."

"Back off, Miller," Travis says, and Miller puts up his hands, winks at me again.

"All right, all right. Go back to your little show-and-tell here," he says. "Hey, listen, there's a party later tonight at Sienna's house. You going?"

Travis shrugs. "We'll see."

Miller grins. "Alternate plans? See you, Lady Sadie."

"Bye." I smile, wave.

Travis looks at me. "I think you've made quite an impression."

"I . . . he never . . . in . . . class. He never even looked at me."

"Yeah, Miller's shy."

I look over at Miller, now shoving some other guy through the door. "You are so dead, Kevin!" he shouts. "I'm gonna pantz you when we get out of here!" The door shuts, and the restaurant is immediately about ten degrees quieter.

❧

"So." Travis guides the car into a dark stretch between the streetlights. "What did you think? Was that so bad?"

I can't help but laugh. "No. It wasn't so bad. Okay, the movie was kind of bad."

"But not the company?" He has taken off his seat belt and has somehow found my hand in the dimness of the car.

"The company was pretty okay," I answer. His thumb traces the shape of my fingers.

"Yeah?"

I don't know where to go in the conversation. I had spent most of the movie noting points that I thought we could talk about, but I used them all up during the car ride. I had offered my opinion that the martial arts parts of the movie were amazing and that the cinematography was beautiful, but that the last scene didn't make sense and that I hadn't liked the main character anyway. Travis had agreed with me on everything.

"Yeah. So do you think that–" But I never have to find out what Travis does think because he leans in, cuts me off with a kiss. And even though I've never done this before, I find it's a relief.

❧

When I let myself into the house, half an hour later, I expect my mother to be pacing the kitchen, my father three steps behind her. But only the empty kitchen table and hum of the dishwasher greet me.

I follow piano music down the hallway, into the living room. My father is standing, one hand resting on my mother's shoulder, the other turning the crinkled pages of a score for her. As far as I know, my mother hasn't played in years, and yet her hands move confidently, expressively across the keys, and the silk strings of music are so sweet that I close my eyes.

Who wants a piano sandwich? I do, I do! Ollie and I try to outscream each other, tumbling and pushing and shoving to smush closer to our mother on the bench. Sometimes we would slip down to the floor and tickle her ankles as she pressed the pedals, the object being who could make her shriek first.

When I open my eyes, my father is watching me. He tilts his head down toward my unsuspecting mother. I smile at him, hold my thumb up in the air, and step backward into the cool darkness of the hallway.

Chapter Twenty

Since I am meeting Lila in an hour, I sketch the ocean in rough and hurried strokes today. When I lean back and squint, I can't even tell what I've drawn, so I close my eyes. The air is cool and wet, smelling of sea grass and rain.

Today will be exactly twelve weeks since we moved. I take a mental inventory. *Friends, check. Boyfriend, maybe check.* Now I just need to work on the part about liking who I am when I'm with him.

"So?" a voice says next to me. My sketchbook tumbles and slides off my legs, lands pages-down in the sand. Ryan is looming over me, on the seawall, blocking out the light. I shift, sit up straight, pick up my book, and try to smooth the sand off the pages. "How was the date?"

I glance at him, look away toward the ocean, which is churning today. I shrug. "It was good."

"Just *good*?" His voice batters down over my head.

"*Great*, then. Can you stop standing over me like that?"

He drops down beside me. Today, his T-shirt is red, with the words TRUST ME, I'M A VIRGIN scrawled across his narrow chest.

"Where do you get these shirts?"

"Mail order. So what did you guys do?"

"Nothing special. We just went out to dinner."

"Where?"

"The Country Squire?" I angle my toes toward Ryan. Even Lila didn't ask me this many questions. I had called her the next morning, but she had sounded distracted, more than usual, and had to get off the phone in less than five minutes.

"Ah, the Country Squire. The bastion of American youth. Did he offer you his jacket afterward?"

"What are you talking about?"

"You know. Are you going steady?"

"Ryan. Does it ever occur to you that you sound like someone's grandmother?"

"Thank you, Sadie. I'll take that as a compliment."

"It wasn't meant as one."

"Still, it's the nicest thing you've ever said to me." His voice is perfectly solemn, his brown eyes earnest behind his glasses, and I search his face to see if he is joking or not. He makes me wait a full minute before the right corner of his mouth slips up and then we are laughing.

I run a finger along the metal spiral of my sketchbook's binding, watch an elderly woman bob her way across the beach. She is dressed in a pink sweat suit, and her hands swing briskly out from her sides.

"So are you going to go out again with him?"

"If he asks."

"*If he asks?* Sadie, Sadie, Sadie, I thought you were a modern woman. You know, you're named after a tradition, Sadie Hawkins Day, where the girl asks the guy to a dance and–"

"I'm named after a great-aunt." I tuck my hair behind my ears, wondering for one minute if Ryan likes my hair, too. "Anyway, next weekend, he said that there was–"

"Let me guess. A birthday party for his best friend, right?"

I stare at Ryan. "How did you–"

Ryan sighs noisily. "It's all so . . . ordinary, isn't it? You go out once to dinner, once to a best friend's birthday party, all of a sudden you're a couple. I mean where are the masked balls?

Where's the mystery? Where's the magic?" He holds his hands in an appeal to the sea, as if trying to find the answer written on the surface of the water.

I laugh, a gulping kind of noise that after a second, I decide doesn't sound real. I take a breath, wait for him to join me, so we can laugh for real again. But he is quiet, resting his chin on bent knees.

I don't want him to be right.

☙

The train clatters and hums into the station. Lila has been silent for the last half hour, her eyes wide, fixed on something I can't see.

I have been studying a smudge of dirt on the back of the seat in front of me. Depending on how much I squint, I can turn it into a two-headed dog or a flower. When I pointed this out to Lila, a smile came and went on her face, brief as a falling star.

Now the train jerks to a halt. All around us passengers begin to depart, mothers holding the hands of small children, fathers following behind, their arms full of shopping bags. But Lila seems poised on her seat, as if waiting for just the right moment to merge into the dwindling mass of human traffic.

I shuffle my feet next to her, and she seems to collect herself.

"Ready?" she says, and I am relieved to hear the word uttered in her usual dry fashion.

"Sure," I say, probably with too much enthusiasm.

She moves toward the doors with her languid grace, and I follow. Once off the train, she turns her head left and right, seems to pick a direction at random, and heads into it.

We had pored over a subway map on the Internet two days before, but now in the rush and clamor of trains and the blare of indecipherable announcements about neglected baggage and lost items, nothing makes sense. Lila stands motionless in the swirl, so I decide that it is up to me. I choose a woman wearing a needle-slim brown tweed skirt and suit jacket, a woman without any children hanging off of her.

"Excuse me."

She is about to click past me, her eyes boring through the air somewhere above my left shoulder, so I try again.

"Please, do you know where the A line is?"

She makes a hurried gesture that I am not sure means anything. "Behind me, down the hallway," she finally relents, and I grab Lila's hand and pull her along.

I swipe the MetroCard that I bought from the vending machine, push through the turnstile, pass the card back to Lila. On the other side of the bars, her face is pale and her lips are moving. She's kind of freaking me out.

"What time is this audition?" I ask, even though I know.

"Two o'clock," she responds. Her lips keep moving.

"Are you talking to yourself?" I ask.

She shakes her head impatiently. "My monologue."

After that, I decide to leave her in silence. I try instead to observe people without having them notice. I watch an old woman hobble up the steps to the subway platform. She is lugging a small cart with three tattered plastic bags stacked inside of it. A middle-aged man overtakes her, bends, murmurs something.

"Just leave me alone. Leave me be, why don't you?" Her voice is crusty and thick, as if not used very often. She makes a swatting motion while heaving her cart up the last two steps.

It wobbles precariously, tips, the bags tumble free, spilling an assortment of empty water bottles, bright red and green soda cans, and a pile of what look like dirty old rags. With a face. I blink. It is a doll, an incredibly dirty doll. It is missing one eye, but its puckered lips are still a deep candy pink. The man's face shifts into polite shock, and he steps around the now-kneeling woman, who has crushed the doll to her shoulder and is crooning softly.

A warm wind stirs through the tunnel, and a minute later, the A train lumbers into view. It is packed with people. The doors slide open and people begin to exit the subway, like puppets, their strings taut. We buffet our way into a car, find a pole to cling to against the lurching motion. Lila's face is still pale. Next to me, a small girl squirms in her seat, sucking at a straw inserted through a large McDonald's cup. In between sucks, she chews the straw and kicks at her little brother until he begins to howl. Their mother, sitting next to them, closes her eyes. The boy slaps the cup out of his sister's hand. Milky gray ribbons of milkshake ooze from the opened lid. The girl screams, a high, piercing shriek.

I look at Lila, ready to roll my eyes. She doesn't seem to have noticed.

❧

When we arrive at the address, there's already a tightly knitted line of people, some talking on cell phones, some talking to each other. Even from across the street, I can pick out extravagant hand gestures and overwrought facial expressions. I study the girls, fascinated.

"They kind of look like you," I blurt out.

"Thanks, Sadie," Lila says. It is the first two words she has spoken since the subway.

"I mean, not really," I try, but anyone can see the obvious truth. They are all tall and slender, with long dark hair. If you grouped them together, they would look like a bunch of sea nymphs or naiads. The background colors would be soft and hazy, to highlight the–

"Sadie." Lila breaks into my reverie, and I startle back to her. Her tone is brisk. "Will you meet me here in, like, two hours?"

"Do you think you'll be done?"

Lila assesses the line. It is starting to ripple as the first sets of people begin to disappear through the now open door. "I think so," she says.

"Don't you want me to wait on line with you?"

She shakes her head, a quick slap of a motion. "No. I'll be okay. Walk around, go shopping, find a coffee shop. Have fun in the big city."

I raise an eyebrow at her, a trick I so recently mastered that I'm not sure if I'm doing it right. "Okay. Knock 'em dead."

"Break a leg," she reminds me patiently.

"Break a leg," I parrot, and blow her a kiss because I am afraid if I hug her, she will pull away. I try to saunter off, try not to feel hurt that she didn't want me with her. I cross the street, look back. Lila has disappeared into the line.

☙

I pace, I check my watch, scan each face, in case Lila is hiding behind some stranger and will step forward saying, "Oh, there you are." I sip at my Styrofoam cup of coffee, its cold, bitter thickness coating my tongue. The line is a lot shorter now and moving forward swiftly. Just as swiftly, people exit from the door, their voices loud, their expressions vibrant.

"Did you hear his delivery?"

"Did he have any expression on his face when you went?"

"I don't know. I fucked up three lines, but I totally felt like I nailed the end. You know that part–"

"Hey," Lila says, materializing at my elbow.

"Hey!" I exclaim. "Where were you?"

"I got out early, went for a walk around the block. Some guy was peeing against a door."

I am not sure how to handle that one. "Um . . . that must have been educational."

She doesn't even smile.

"How did it go?"

She shrugs a very Lila shrug, one shoulder up, pause, down. "It went."

"Do you think you got it? Do you think–"

"I don't know. Mind if we walk back to the station? I feel like a walk."

"Sure." My voice is soft. I am afraid of breaking something.

We cross the street in silence and begin walking uptown. All around, people are hurrying off to their own destinations. They grip their bags and briefcases, push through with elbows jutting out from their bodies. Lila blends in with them, walking swiftly, her left arm swinging outward a little.

Finally, I catch up with her at the crosswalk. Taxis skim past us, their yellow lights blinking off and on. A giant hot dog dances on the opposite street corner, thrusting green flyers into people's faces as they dodge around him. "Look," I say, nudging Lila, pointing him out to her.

"What?" she asks abruptly.

"Hey," I say, and then in a whisper, "Lila?"

She turns and buries her face in my neck, and I wrap my arms around her, feeling her spine pitch with the force of her sobs. "He didn't even let me get through half of my monologue. It was so *brutal.* He just cut me off and said, 'Thank you very much, Miss Harrison,' and that was it. He couldn't even get my name right. It was right there in front of him on my résumé, and he couldn't even get my fucking name right. That was it, Sadie."

"It's okay, it's okay, it's okay," I say, tugging at her. We stumble into the shelter of a padlocked, recessed doorway. I watch green flyers skip and tumble past us on the breeze. "There'll be other auditions, there–"

Lila lifts her head. The skin around her nose is a chapped pink color. "What if they're all like that, Sadie? What if nothing ever happens to me? What if I never get anywhere?"

"That's not going to happen. This was just one bad experience, okay? *Okay?*" I shake her a little. "This guy just didn't know. He didn't know, Lila. He didn't know about you."

But I don't think she can even hear me, she is crying so hard.

❧

The sun is setting behind me as I let myself back into the house, wide swaths of apricot and peach staining the fading blue. When we were little, Ollie and I were convinced that a giant came every evening with an enormous paintbrush, dripping with golden-red paint, to cover the sky.

Something is sizzling, and a waft of spicy, slightly burnt-smelling steam greets me. My mother is standing at the stove, staring down at the large wok that she and my father rescued yesterday at their latest tag sale. I notice that she is wearing her chili apron that my father gave her last Christmas, although something brown has spilled down the front of it, obscuring two of the chilies.

She looks up at me, smiles distractedly. "We're having Szechwan Surprise," she announces, then hunches back over her cookbook. "And your father is going to be a little late, so I think we might eat without him."

Lucky him. I head to the refrigerator to find a Coke. I pop the tab, drink deeply, the sweet soda fizzing over my tongue. I lower the can to encounter my mother's disapproving eyes.

"At least put it in a glass. You know, I read a report on how dirty the tops of those cans really are. The germs . . ."

I hold up the can, tip it a little so the remaining liquid sloshes from side to side. "I don't want any more, anyway. Do you want the rest?"

My mother shakes her head, a small fastidious movement. I pour the rest of the can into the sink, watching the liquid foam down the drain, expecting a lecture on the waste of it all. I have several replies prepared, so when she does speak, she catches me by surprise.

"Your friend Travis called for you."

I turn, the can dropping from my fingers. It bounces across the floor.

"He was very polite. He asked for you, and then asked if he could please leave a message, and he asked how I was."

"He's very polite," I find myself echoing inanely.

"Anyway," she continues, "he left his number. I put it by the phone."

"Thanks, Mom." I kiss her on the cheek, look down at the contents of the wok, which are furiously bubbling away like some science experiment gone wrong.

Chapter Twenty-One ❧

"Yeah, but really, how many times have you seen a pretty girl with bad teeth?" Lila is asking Christie as I walk into English class the next morning. She flips the glossy pages of *Elle.* "See, you don't see her teeth at all here."

"And she looks good," Christie interjects.

"Yeah, but look at *this* picture." Lila glances up at me as I take my seat next to her, mutters, "Caldwell, save me."

Christie's cell phone buzzes, and with a surreptitious look toward the front of the room, she answers it.

"You don't need saving," I answer Lila, but she just waves off my words. She seems back to normal, meeting my eyes with no hesitation. I pull out my copy of *The Tempest.* This is our third Shakespeare play in a row, and who knows if it's our last, since Snore refuses to give out a syllabus or answer any questions. "Has this become a Shakespeare-only class, by the way?"

"Shhhh," Lila says, puts one slender finger to her lips, widens her eyes dramatically. She indicates our teacher, who has his head bent over his attendance book as if something is puzzling him. "You'll hurt Snore's feelings. All he ever wanted to be was a Shakespearean actor."

I lean closer, lower my voice. "So what happened? Hey, you wouldn't consider ever teaching acting if you–" I gulp under her glare. "Sorry!"

"Would *you* like to be a high school art teacher like Big Byrd?" Her voice is slathered in scorn.

"Well . . ." I consider this. "Would I have to wear those caftans all the time?"

Lila snorts. "Probably. You and I, Caldwell, are destined for better things. I've decided."

"Oh, really?" I rest my head against the wall, listening intently.

"Yeah. I've got it all planned out. You and me, we're going to go to New York City after we graduate."

I risk it. "You had so much fun there yesterday that–"

But she continues, undaunted. "That was a rehearsal. Not even a dress rehearsal. So listen. We get a little apartment, probably in the midst of a crack den, so it's not too expensive, and you'll paint all day and I'll–"

"Recite monologues to me while I paint?"

"Maybe."

"And maybe we could–"

"Hey," Lila interrupts suddenly. "Lover boy is looking lost out there." I follow the direction of her gaze. Through the open doorway, I see Travis. He waves at me, beckons. "Have you seen him since your date on Friday?"

I shake my head, stumble to my feet, look at the wall clock. There's five minutes before the first bell will ring.

"Ah, playing hard to get. Very wise, Caldwell. I didn't think you had it in you, but–"

"Shut up." Then I turn to her anxiously. "Do you think he thinks that? I mean, we talked on the phone yesterday, not for that long, but I had to eat dinner and–"

"I think he's going to think that if you leave him hanging in the doorway, you idiot. Go. And your face is red," she adds kindly. I want to kick her.

I make my way discreetly through the row of desks with my head down, managing not to look at Snore as I escape the room.

Travis is leaning against the wall, just outside the door. "Hi," I whisper.

"Hi," he whispers back, takes my hand, folds it against his chest. He is wearing a soft-looking button-down shirt, and I want to trace my fingers across the stripes.

"So . . . how are you?"

"Pretty good. And yourself?"

I nod. "Good." Then I think about what else to say. "Now."

And this is apparently the right thing, because he smiles, steps in closer, and kisses me. I rest my free hand on his shoulder, feel his muscles tighten briefly under my fingers. Then his tongue touches mine and I stop thinking.

"If Miss Caldwell has finished her tête-à-tête in the hallway, perhaps she might care to join us for the small-utterly-inconvenient-and-I'm-sure-rather-less-fascinating matter of English class." Snore's voice is icily polite, and I look at my teacher, dazed.

He raises an eyebrow at me, stands aside, and gestures expansively into the classroom.

"I have to go," I whisper to the third button on Travis's shirt.

"I'll see you at lunch," Travis answers, touches the back of my neck lightly, walks away.

"Sorry," I murmur to my teacher as I scurry through the door. I make my way past a blur of faces, fall into my seat.

"Act three, scene five, please," Snore intones, and there is a soft rustle of pages. "This is the scene between Miranda and Ferdinand. Remember, this is the first blush of love." Someone snickers, falls immediately silent as Snore's eyes swivel across the room. I focus on my paperback copy of the play in front of me, on what appears to be a tomato-sauce stain on the right-hand corner of the page.

"Perhaps, Miss Caldwell, you would like to read the part of Miranda?"

❧

Ryan saunters into Driver's Ed ten minutes after the class has started, and I think Coach Vesecki is going to combust. Oblivious, Ryan takes the empty seat between me and the guy who I'm beginning to think has a sleep disorder, since at the start of class, he pushed his baseball cap over his face and started breathing deeply.

We all wait for Coach Vesecki to resume lecturing. Which he does after a very long and pointed silence.

"Driving in adverse conditions," Coach Vesecki says. "Who can tell me about adverse conditions?"

I raise my hand.

"Yes, Sadie?"

"Snow, sleet, rain, ice?"

"Yes. All very adverse conditions. Good."

Ryan raises his hand, but Coach Vesecki ignores him, turns back to the board, carefully prints each of my words in clumsy block letters.

"Now," Coach Vesecki continues, "who can tell me the rules of driving in adverse conditions?" He glances out at us again, takes in Ryan's still-raised hand.

"Yes?"

"What about road rage?"

"What about it?"

"Isn't that an adverse condition?"

"Not technically–"

"But *adverse* is synonymous with *antagonistic*, and road rage is perpetuated by antagonistic drivers, therefore, wouldn't road rage be an adverse condition?" Ryan pauses, adds in a persuasive tone, "I just want to make sure I know all the adverse conditions."

Coach Vesecki stares at him, his face darkening.

I focus on the flatly colored photo in my book of a man and a woman sitting in the front seat of a car. The man is looking out the driver's-side window at the billowing clouds in the sky. When I look up again, Coach has turned back to the board, and Ryan is serenely balancing a piece of paper on the sleeping guy's head.

❧

"You know all the famous artists starved before they were successful," Lila insists as we position ourselves on the volleyball court. All week, she has been mapping out more of our post–high school lives.

"*You* would not be able to starve." I keep my eye on the white blob of the volleyball, praying it won't come anywhere near me.

"I can starve if I have to," Lila insists. She reaches up a casual, closed fist, punches the ball into a high arc. I watch a short girl wearing black leggings jump valiantly for it and miss.

Mrs. Osborne blows her whistle. "Point!" she shrieks.

"Yeah, but . . ." I watch the ball snag in the net on the other side. It bounces once, twice on the floor before the short girl scoops it up and passes it back to the server, a taller girl, her face gripped by a look of fierce determination.

"You have to go to college," Erica chimes in. She is playing the net because she is particularly good at spiking.

"I don't have to," Lila says mildly.

"Everyone goes to college."

"No," Lila says, her voice informative, thoughtful. "No, Erica, not everyone goes to college. Some of us are not lucky enough to afford it."

"Yeah, but . . ." Erica falters. "Scholarships."

Lila laughs with genuine amusement. "Who would give me a scholarship? For real?"

The ball sails over my head, and I swat at it feebly. "Sadie, look alive there!" Mrs. Osborne calls, blows her whistle again.

❧

"What's wrong with this picture?" Ruth says in a muted semiwail.

I study her painting. "Your bananas. Definitely the bananas need work."

She gives me a despairing eye roll. "I haven't even *started* the bananas yet."

I examine her picture again. "That explains why they don't look like bananas."

She sighs, stabs her brush against her palette, and I refrain from commenting on how she is ruining the bristles. "Three more minutes," she murmurs, looks over her shoulder, shudders. "God, he is so creepy."

Ryan is sitting behind an empty easel in the far corner of the room. I can see the top of his head, bent over the straight lines of his book, his hands gripping each cover. He is reading with a concentration that borders on intense.

"He's not doing anything," I say quietly, staring at my picture again. I have finished with the bunch of bananas and am now trying to get the edge of the table to take on the proper angles.

"He was. A minute ago."

"What?"

"Showing me his tongue." She whips the word *tongue* at me, and I can't help it. I laugh. Then I take in her flushed cheeks and feel immediately sorry.

"Just ignore him," I say in my best soothing voice, and shoot Ryan a look.

The bell rings. Ruth tears her picture off the easel with a flourish. "Coming?" she asks, untying her smock and pulling it over her head.

I shrug. "I just want to finish this one part. I'll be there soon."

She hesitates. "Are you sure? What if Travis is looking for you?"

I stop, wonder if there is some rule I am breaking. "He can find me here if he wants."

But she still looks worried, cuts her eyes over to Ryan. "I'll be there soon," I promise, trying not to let any impatience soak into my voice, and finally Ruth nods, picks up her bag, and ducks out through the stand of easels.

I wait until the room clears, until Mrs. Byrd steps out into the hallway to monitor the traffic. Then I glance sideways. This time, Ryan looks up from his book.

"You know," he calls from across the room. "It occurs to me that we're like Zola and Cézanne."

I nod thoughtfully, slowly. He raises one eyebrow at me. "You do know who I'm talking about, right?"

I consider his raised eyebrow, the way his arms are folded loosely across his chest, and know that I can't get away with lying. "Sort of. No. Cézanne, of course, yes."

"Points for you there at least."

"I'm so relieved your opinion of me hasn't totally tanked." My voice is dry, nonchalant, my best Lila impression, which must not be too good because Ryan seems unabashed.

"Cézanne, the painter–"

"I know who he was–"

"And Émile Zola, the writer, were great friends at the time of the art salon in Paris."

"And you are Zola because . . ." I dip my brush, try for the play of shadows along a fold of the red scarf that Mrs. Byrd has flung dramatically across the table. The bristles slide across the page. There is silence. I look over. Ryan is reading again.

"Hey," I say. "We're having a conversation here. You are Zola because you want to be a writer?"

Ryan taps his chin with one finger. "I don't want to be a writer. I just want to write."

"That makes no sense."

"Okay, it doesn't."

"It sounds kind of pseudo-ish coming from you."

He splays one hand over his heart, closes his eyes. "You wound me."

I turn back to my painting, frown at it. "So . . . you write?" I ask, outlining another fold of the scarf with delicate strokes.

"A little. Maybe. Yeah."

I am careful now not to look at him. "Poetry?"

"Poetry, plays, some short stories."

"All your own?" I ask casually, and stand back. The angle of my scarf is not true enough. I step in again.

"All my own," he answers, obviously puzzled.

"Really? So you would never write another poet's words, like Kipling's, for example, up on . . . oh, I don't know, a wall?"

And I am rewarded by Ryan's genuine laugh. "Did you know those lines already?"

"I hate to disappoint you *again.* I had to look them up online."

He shrugs, still pleased. "Yeah, Andy really didn't appreciate that too much. I had to stop."

"Can I read something, sometime? Something of your own?"

"Ifyoulike." Ryan says this all in a rush. He is bent over his book again, staring at it.

"I would like," I say softly.

❧

After my last class, I duck into the Drama and Art wing, looking for Lila. I hadn't seen her at lunch, and I feel restless. But the auditorium is empty except for Snore, who is pacing the stage, notebook in hand, muttering. I duck back behind the wide double doors as Snore stops, stares out into the audience. Suddenly, he tosses aside his notebook, and it flips through the air, white pages flashing briefly, before landing with a *thunk* on the stage. Snore doesn't even seem to register that. Instead, he pumps his arms through the air as if arguing with some imaginary foe.

"He's lost it," Lila says behind me, and I whirl, so happy to see her.

"Hi, you weren't at lunch today." I say all in a rush. "I missed you!"

She raises an eyebrow, grins. "Lover boy wasn't enough to keep you occupied? You better have a word with him."

We linger in the doorway next to each other, watching Snore, who has now dropped to his knees, pleading with the invisible someone.

"Rumor has it, he was some stage actor in New York for a while," Lila says, her voice hushed. "And that he walked out in the middle of a production of *Hamlet*. Just left the theater."

"Was he playing Hamlet?"

"Yes."

"No, no, no!" Snore expostulates wildly, still on his knees. I jump. Our teacher has clapped one arm across his face. The other is outstretched before him as if to ward off some unspeakable evil.

Lila stirs. "I gotta get in there before he launches into his 'To Be or Not to Be' speech. That always puts him in a mood." She shifts her backpack to her other shoulder. "Oh, this Friday, there's a Hitchcock revival at the Bradley. Starts with *Psycho,* ends with *Rear Window*. If you haven't seen *Rear Window*, you have had a seriously flawed upbringing. You want to come with me?"

I hesitate. "I think Travis said something about . . . some birthday party for a friend of his."

Lila shrugs. "Okay."

"But I want to come with you. I do. Maybe I can–"

"I'll eat some popcorn for you."

"Lila," I say swiftly. "I'll come with you. I'll tell Travis–"

"Sadie," she says, surprised. "It's okay. Go to the birthday party with him. It'll be fun."

I don't answer at first. Then, "Have you ever dated anyone?" I take a tiny breath.

But Lila doesn't seem mad. "Who?" she asks, almost cheerfully. "Who in this dump of a place would I date?"

"Well, that guy who likes you, you know, the one Erica calls . . . Theater . . . Geek?" My voice trails away. "You're so pretty. A lot of guys like you."

"Oh, really?" Lila says. Her voice has deepened into her Southern drawl. "Where *are* they?" She slips through the doorway, starts down the aisle, turns back. "Besides, I don't want to get stuck at birthday parties," she adds, blows me a kiss, proceeds up to the stage, where Snore is staring at nothing at all.

❧

Travis wraps his arms around me and I sway against him, even though the music is loud and fast. But he seems to like this slow dance in the middle of the room, and so do I. He swigs from a bottle of beer, offering me sips now and then. It tastes warm and smoky and makes me thirsty. I decline after the third sip. Just when I am thinking it would be easy to stay like this forever, the music stops.

"Yo, Travis." We pull apart a little. At the far end of the living room, Miller is standing next to the band. He is wearing a Happy Birthday hat, and it slides down one side of his face as he churns his arm in the "come over here" signal. "When you gonna play for us?" he calls.

"All right, all right." Travis kisses the top of my head, moves off. "Take it easy," he adds, as if Miller and the rest of the band were planning to start a riot.

I adjust the silver bangles on my wrist, teetering a little in the vintage rhinestone high heels I borrowed from Lila. Somehow, she manages to walk in them as if they were sneakers. I wish she were here. Even if all she would do is announce that the music sucks.

Travis bends over the bass guitar, his hands moving up and down the frets as he tunes it. He jangles out a chord, goes back to tuning. He looks good up there, and I notice more than a few girls gathering near that end of the room. I glance at the archway into the kitchen, thinking to go find a Coke, when I see Erica, also standing by herself. If she notices me, she gives no sign. I think for a minute, then make my way over, trying not to wobble.

"Hi," I say, coming to a stop next to her. "What are you drinking?"

"Gin and tonic." While her voice is not exactly friendly, it's not exactly cold, either.

"That's cool," I say. "Having fun?"

She shrugs. "It's okay. You?"

"Yeah."

"I bet."

"Erica," I begin. "I'm sorry about Travis and me."

She studies me with eyes underscored by black liner. "Are you?"

"I thought you said you were over him . . . I didn't . . ." There's no way to proceed. No way to explain. She will hate me forever.

But unexpectedly she says, "It's cool, Sadie. There was never anything anyway." Her voice is offhand, lacking malice, and I must look as astonished as I feel, because she frowns at me. "*What?* I had a crush on him, like, briefly, forever ago. So don't give me that."

"Okay, okay," I say mildly. We watch Travis and Miller, still at the front of the room, now talking to a third guy, who is fiddling with the amp.

"Are they ever going to play?" Erica asks, as if I am the authority.

"Soon. So, hey," I begin casually. "What do you think of Miller?"

Erica touches a fingertip to one of her earrings. "Why?"

"Nothing," I say, drawing out the word.

"Tell me," she insists. She raises her plastic cup as if to drink, but then does not.

"He thinks you're cute."

"He said that?" She turns to face me fully.

I backtrack. "Not to me. To Travis."

She digests this in silence, gives a more considering look toward the front of the room.

"I like your heels," she says, takes a final sip of her drink. She pulls the lime wedge from the cup, nibbles at it.

"Thanks. They're Lila's."

"I know."

Chapter Twenty-Two

On Sunday, dusk finds me still on the beach. I huddle inside my jacket, with my sketchpad open, even though the light is fading. But I can draw the ocean by heart now, having done it at least a thousand times. I move my charcoal across the page unerringly; this time, I am adding little caps of waves, since the November wind has picked up. Two people, their arms wrapped around each other's waists, bob along the edge of the shore, their joined gait shuffling and ungainly. It looks like a hard way to walk.

"The mermaid returns to the ocean," Ryan says suddenly, dropping down next to me. My hand twitches and my pencil skitters across the page. I frown down at the light charcoal line slipping jagged off the edge of the page. I resist the urge to slam the sketchbook closed, wait under his scrutiny.

"You draw the ocean a lot," he says at last. "Why?"

I set my pencil and book aside, bury my fingers in cold sand. "No reason."

"There is a reason," Ryan persists.

I look sideways at him. Through the open V of his long black trench coat, I read GOD IS DEAD, written in jagged white letters on a bright blue background. "Why do you always wear those shirts?" I ask now.

His gaze remains steady on me until I look away.

"I wear them because I want people to notice."

"Do they?"

"What do you think? Why do you always wear that?"

"What?"

"That." And his fingers, light as water, find the dog tag hanging around my neck.

I pull away, my hand cupping protectively over the small piece of metal.

"Memento?" he quips.

"Something like that."

"Hey," he says, as if he just remembered something. "I brought you a poem. Of mine. If you still want to read it." He fumbles through his pocket, takes out a piece of paper that has been folded many times. He takes a piece of blue-gray lint from a corner of it. "Here," he says, thrusts the paper toward me.

"Thanks." I tuck the paper carefully into my sketchbook.

"Want this, too?" he asks, holds out the piece of lint.

I can't help but laugh. "I'm good, thanks."

We settle into silence for a few minutes.

"So why do you always draw–"

"The ocean? I try to draw it every day. Even though it's impossible."

"Why is it impossible?" Ryan asks, his fingers fiddling with the laces of his combat boots.

The wind picks up and the tattered remains of a white plastic bag briefly take flight. "It just is. You can't draw the whole ocean. It's always changing."

"So you try to stop it from changing?"

"No. Not exactly. . . . I made a promise to my brother that I would draw the ocean for him for the rest of my life."

"Your brother? He doesn't go to our school. Is he younger than you?"

"No. Yes. Not exactly." I scoop some hair out of my eyes, hold it away from my face with one hand. Lights are beginning to blink on in the houses to my right. I can feel Ryan's unwavering intensity, so I stare straight ahead at the vast ocean, gray and cold and constantly alive. "He's dead. He died when we were twelve. He was . . . is my twin."

I wait for Ryan's inevitable next question.

"Is?" His voice is very soft.

"I still see him. Physically. Sometimes. Whenever he wants to appear. I don't know. I never questioned it. I was just so happy when he first came back to me." A seagull shrieks overhead, a brief, lonely, wild sound. I close my eyes. "So you think I'm really weird, right?" I ask. Suddenly, I am furious. I look at him directly, challenging. "If you do, that'd be hilarious coming from someone like you." I brush my hands off on my jeans, short, sharp motions.

"Someone like me?" And now the usual mockery is back in Ryan's voice.

"Yeah. Like you. *Fryin'* Ryan." We glare at each other. "Why did you do it anyway?"

"Do what?"

"Lie to people like that? Say your father was really a mass murderer who was going to be electrocuted."

"Oh, that," Ryan says, and waves his hand in the air as if bored with my question.

"Yes, *that.* It's really screwed up."

"That's hilarious coming from someone like *you.*"

In the failing light, we run out of words. Ryan half lunges toward me, grabs the back of my neck in a sort of tackle. He presses his lips to the side of my mouth, his face cold against mine. I turn my head, note a fissure running deep in the wall. We pull away and, almost as an afterthought, I raise my hand and slap him, not hard, catching the edge of his jaw. "Travis," I remind Ryan accusingly, throwing down the name like a shield, even though we both know it's not true.

Ryan shakes his head, as if he has water in his ear, a minor annoyance, but I notice he won't meet my eyes.

I spring to my feet, snatch up my sketchbook. My pencil is buried somewhere in the sand, but I am not about to dig for it. "Don't try that again," I call as I walk toward the steps carved into the seawall. I wait for a response from him. Something, anything.

But it never comes.

Chapter Twenty-Three

"Did you see the set of wheels Fryin' Ryan's got?" Erica says, as she sits down at the lunch table, pulls out a plastic bag of carrot sticks. She holds out the bag to us, and Travis takes one, eats it in two snapping bites.

"He can't."

Travis and Erica look at me.

"I mean, he's still in Driver's Ed with me. We finish the class at the end of this week."

"Maybe he passed," Erica says.

"No, you have to finish the course before you get your license. That's–"

"It's a MINI Cooper, red, with a white stripe."

Travis whistles. "Those are sweet. That's my next car."

Erica chews, swallows. "I bet it's not his."

I stare at her, at her mouth set so primly around her carrot. "I don't think he's a car thief, Erica," I snap.

She gives me a wounded look. "Okay, Sadie. What's it to you, anyway?"

"Nothing." I lean back in my chair. "Sorry." I push my knee into Travis's knee, feeling relieved when he smiles at me. I smile back, scan the lunch room, looking for Lila. Instead, I see Miller lumbering toward us.

"Yo, Travis!" he bellows from ten feet away. As he passes Mrs. Sneed, who is on lunchroom duty today, she gives a little shudder, wraps her pale blue cardigan more tightly around her shoulders. Miller comes to a stop at our table, and he and Travis exchange a complicated handshake, complete with smashing their bare knuckles into each other's three times in rapid succession. Then Miller kicks free a chair, sits down.

"Ladies," he says after a minute, stares at Erica, who looks away. "So, what's up?"

"We're talking about Freakshow's new car," Travis says casually. "Did you see it? The MINI?"

Miller lets out a hoot. "That's *his*? Get out of here! I was checking that one out in the parking lot this morning." He frowns. "What's Freakshow doing with a car like that? No way they could afford that."

Travis rocks his chair back. "On a police officer's salary? How much do they make, anyway?"

"We think it's stolen," Erica says to Miller, and now her voice skips a little with excitement.

"*I* don't," I say, but Miller doesn't pay attention.

"Relax, Sadie," Travis whispers to me. "She's kidding." He pulls me over in a one-armed hug. I bend against the awkward angle, say nothing.

"Stolen?" Miller repeats. "Seems like Freakshow's got quite the criminal streak." He stares up at the ceiling.

"What do you mean?" Travis asks the question just before I do.

"He's the one who spray-painted that shit in the locker room."

"The poetry?" I ask, trying to sound surprised.

Miller nods. "Yeah. Coach just told me that." He whistles, a long-drawn-out, tuneless sound. "I always wanted me one of those MINIs."

Something about his voice makes me sit up straighter.

Under the table, Ollie taps my ankle three times, our warning signal.

❧

"Sadie!"

I spatter indigo paint across the edge of my canvas. Ryan is standing by my easel.

"Did the–"

"I need your help." Ryan cuts me off. He looks different somehow, and after a minute, I realize his glasses are gone. I take in the rest of his appearance. The sleeve on his coat is torn and soaked. There is a red mark high up on the left side of his face, just under his eye.

"What happened to you?"

"Does your boyfriend know where my car is?"

"What?"

"Your boyfriend, tall, football player guy–"

"Does Travis know *what*?"

"My car. Is. Missing. The football team. Is. Responsible. And your boyfriend, being on the football team, might have an idea or three that he'd share with you."

"What happened to you?" I ask again, set down my paintbrush.

"My car is gone. From the parking lot."

I touch his coat sleeve. He pulls back, looks at me with exasperation. "No. Travis didn't do this. It was these other guys in the bathroom. I don't even remember their names, they all look alike."

Somehow I doubt that Ryan doesn't know their names, but I stay silent.

"They said they weren't . . . going to steal it. Like I did. Just borrow it for a while. They got the keys away from me." He swallows.

"You can't even drive," I say. "And I mean legally, Ryan. You haven't passed the course yet. You didn't even show up for the test last week." And then frustrated that he won't crack, I ask, "Whose car is it?"

"My father's–"

"That's okay, then . . ."

Ryan shakes his head. "My father's friend's. He was keeping it for the weekend for him. Apparently, my mom wants one really bad, so my dad was going to take her for a drive tomorrow night."

I study him for a minute, transfer my brush from my palette to the small plastic cup of water perched on the edge of my easel. "Why?" I ask at last.

Ryan pulls his glasses from his coat pocket and begins to carefully, laboriously straighten the frames. But his fingers are shaking, and so I take them from him, bend them delicately until they look about right.

"I wanted to . . . offer you a ride home."

My hands still. "You wanted to . . . so you stole a car?"

"Borrowed."

"Stole," I insist.

He tries for a smile. "When you hear Vesecki's speech enough . . . you know the one?"

"You mean that part where 'a girl will look at a guy with a little more respect if he has a car'–that crap?"

"Gee, I kind of wish I knew you felt that way *before* I stole the car." He takes his glasses back from me, but makes no move to put them on.

Something is niggling at me. "But wait a minute, you weren't even there for that speech. You walked in late–"

"I'm kind of a repeat offender in that class, remember? He makes the same speech every session. Trust me." He puts on his glasses, looks around the room as if checking all angles of sight.

Then he says, "So, will you help me?"

"Travis," I begin. "He's at practice. He . . . yes. I'll help you."

❧

Deep into the woods, we find the car. I find it first, but Ryan is right behind me. I feel him stop short, but I can't turn. The car is covered in shaving cream and streamers and pictures that look like they came straight from a centerfold.

"Well," I say, feeling my face start to burn in the cold November air. "We found it."

I step forward, pick up a leaf from the ground and clear a semicircle through the shaving cream. I lean down, peer through the windshield. Nothing seems to have been damaged inside the car. The keys are on the front seat.

Ryan's face is wooden, and I wonder if he is thinking of his father.

This intense silence is beginning to make me nervous, so I slide behind the steering wheel. The engine starts smoothly, unlike Lila's Beetle's. The air around me still holds that new-car smell, so I fumble at the controls until a window slides down. A curl of shaving cream drips onto the interior of the door, and I wipe it away with my sleeve. I lean out, look at Ryan. He reminds me of nothing more than a balloon that has lost all its air.

"See, it's fine," I say finally. "It's working."

"Yeah?" His voice is subdued. Slowly, he treks around to the passenger side of the car, opens the door, slumps next to me.

"We just need to clean it up a little," I continue, trying for practical. "We'll get some rags and paper towels from the art room. And some sponges and buckets–"

"Listen, thanks, Sadie. I'll take it from here." His voice is super light, a return to the usual, but I notice the way his hands clutch at the edge of the seat.

"Ryan," I begin. My knee brushes up against the keys, and they clang out a faint metallic protest. "I don't . . . I'm trying to be your friend."

"Why are you my friend only on the beach?" And suddenly his voice shifts into bleak.

"We're not on the beach now, are we?"

"We're in the woods. Same thing. Why are you my friend only when no one else is around?"

I stare out the windshield at the maple tree directly in front of us. Yellow-and-orange scraps of leaves spiral down to adhere to the snow-white shaving cream that covers the hood of the car. I don't have an answer I want to give, so I try a Ryan tactic.

"Why did you lie to everyone in seventh grade about your father?"

His sharp sigh fills the interior of the car, and I think he's not going to speak, but then he surprises me. "I don't know."

"You do know."

"I . . . did you ever wish you could be different?"

"Yeah. All the time. I wish I would stop being so weird."

Ryan looks at me. "I don't think you are."

"I talk to my *dead* brother, Ryan."

He shrugs. "Weird's relative."

"Coming from you, that's very comforting." But I am smiling as I say this. I find the button to recline my seat, push backward, fold my arms, settle in. I wait one full minute by the dashboard clock, then start tapping my fingers on the steering wheel. Ryan takes the hint.

"Okay. It was seventh grade. We were having a debate in our Social Studies class about the death penalty, and everyone was agreeing with the teacher that it was just absolutely wrong and what if someone was innocent and . . . anyway, I just wanted people to think. That's *all* I want, Sadie, I swear. I want people to think for once. Just think about things other than their small little lives, think about greater issues instead of their iPods and who fucked whom last night at this party and what college we're all going to. Okay?"

He looks at me fiercely, and I nod.

"So," Ryan says after a minute. "I said that my own father was a mass murderer and that he had killed eleven people in a bank robbery and that he was about to be executed next Saturday, and what did everyone think about that? It didn't matter that I actually *don't* believe in the death penalty, I just wanted people to stop nodding along with whatever crap we're being fed from the front of the room. I wanted people to *talk* about something. Something real."

"So then they found out?"

"Yeah." Ryan slouches back in his seat, his coat bunching around him. "The guidance counselor called my parents in, there was this big deal about it. And everyone pretty much stopped talking to me."

"And your parents?" I ask softly.

"Yeah, they did, too. Not my mom so much as my dad."

"And now?"

Ryan's eyes are too bright. "Who has a perfect relationship with their parents, anyway? It's character-building."

We look out through the windshield in silence. Watching the slow drift of leaves, I imagine that the car is really a boat, that we might sail away through the thicket of trees at any moment.

❧

The plan is that Ryan will drive us to his house and we'll scrub down the car, getting rid of all traces of shaving cream and toilet paper. But when he pulls into the driveway, from the way our speed suddenly slackens until we are crawling, I know something's not good.

The house is a long, narrow ranch-style, painted a crisp white, with a tiny oblong yard. Someone has planted mums all around the edges of the walkway, their brave yellow blooms holding out against the first frost. A Chevy pickup, black paint peeling off the side, is parked in the strip of graveled driveway.

"What's wrong?"

"My dad's home already. Shit." His voice is matter-of-fact. I look through the half-moon path that the windshield wipers have managed to clear, toward the man who is waiting on the front steps. He is wearing a blue padded jacket and his arms are crossed. For some reason, I don't remember him being this tall even when he was looming at Lila's window just two months ago. I squirm down in my seat, hoping I am hidden by the splotches of shaving cream and shreds of toilet paper.

"We who are about to die salute you," Ryan murmurs, opens the door, gets out of the car.

"Hi, Dad," he calls, his voice oddly cheerful. Slowly, slowly, Ryan's father unfolds his arms, comes down the steps. His face is windburned red.

"What did you think you were doing?" he asks, his voice brusque.

Ryan turns his palms skyward, and I can't imagine what he can answer to that.

"Why. Did. You. Do. Something. So. Stupid?" Each word is bitten down to the quick.

I slide farther down in my seat.

"And what is all this?" He points at the car.

"Ah . . . little trouble at school. Just a prank."

"Who?"

"I don't know. It's not a big deal. Just silly stuff–"

"Who?" The word is relentless as rain.

"I don't *know*, Dad."

"I want these kids' numbers. I'm tired of this. And you shouldn't be letting this happen to yourself. You should–"

I climb out of my side of the car. Ryan's father swings his head, pins me in his sights. I pray he's pulled over 125 speeders since Lila and me, and that cops don't necessarily *have* to have the longest of memories.

"Hi," I say, opening my hand briefly into a wave.

Ryan's father's face is still hard, but he manages to collect himself and say, "Good afternoon."

"I'm–"

"This is my friend, Sadie." Ryan extends one arm in my direction, and I walk over to stand beside him. "Sadie, this is my dad."

I smile. "Nice to meet you. Um . . . should we get started?" I look at Ryan's father. "I came to help Ryan clean up the car," I say, wishing I didn't sound so childish.

"Oh," Ryan's father says, and then again, "Oh. Well . . ."

"It was a joke at school," I say. "A lot of cars got this. A lot."

Ryan's father looks back at Ryan. "Really?" he says, and I can tell he doesn't believe me in the slightest. But now the corners of his mouth are slipping upward. "You go to school with Ryan?"

I nod. "Yes, sir."

"Sadie's an artist," Ryan blurts out.

"Is that so?"

"Yeah. I told her we're like Zola and Cézanne."

"Oh, really?" Ryan's father says politely, and I can tell he hopes this is a compliment. "Well. Listen, Sadie, you don't have to help clean up the car. Ryan and I can handle that."

"Dad," Ryan says, and now his voice is more urgent. "If it's okay, I'd like to walk Sadie home. I'll come right back."

I don't say anything as Ryan's father considers this, his face working with some deeply held emotion.

"It's a little ways. She lives on the beach. But I'll come right back." I have never heard Ryan so serious or so entreating.

"And then we are going to have a talk," his father says finally. "Okay. You make sure she gets home safe." He clears his throat, holds out his hand. "It was a pleasure to meet you, Sadie."

"You, too, sir," I squeak.

We walk down the driveway in silence, and I wait until we reach the edge of it before I dare to look at Ryan.

There is a grin escaping the edges of his mouth. "Shit, you blew my father's mind when you got out of the car. He was like, 'Thank God, my son might actually be normal. Stealing a car, bringing home a girl.'"

"Oh, God, I know! Did you see the look on his face?" I wrap my arms around myself, giddy.

We walk in easy silence through tree-lined blocks of houses that are gradually spaced farther and farther apart. Our breath curls out before us and the sky dims from blue to purple-gray. I smell the first hint of salt air, and as we turn onto my lane, Ryan says, "Listen, Sadie." His face is serious again. "That thing I said earlier, that you're my friend only on the beach. I'm sorry."

"Sorry for what?"

Ryan shrugs, rearranges some gravel on my driveway with the blunt curve of his combat boot. "Nothing. See you later, okay?" He walks away, and I half expect him to turn at the edge of my driveway, call back something Ryan-ish. But he doesn't.

"Sorry for what?" I ask Ollie, who has shadowed us all the way home.

Chapter Twenty-Four

"Mom," I call as I swing through the kitchen door. Shaving cream has stained the cuffs of my jacket, and I strip it off in the foyer, head into the laundry room off the kitchen. Sheets and towels churn in the dryer. I bury my jacket in the waiting laundry basket and continue through the house.

"I'm home. Sorry I'm late, I was working on this end-of-term project in the art room." I take the steps two at a time to my room.

My mother is standing by my desk, her hand resting on a stack of folded jeans and shirts, as if she has just deposited it on my dresser. Somehow, though, I get the feeling that she's been standing there for hours. "Hi," I say, my voice slipping up at the end into a question. "What–"

"This letter came for you. From the school." She removes her hand from the laundry pile and motions toward my desk, then returns her hand to the same exact position, as if the laundry will fall if she doesn't monitor it. I look at my desk, at the neatly slit-open envelope, at the return address with the Driver's Ed logo on it over Pioneer High's address. It's hard to tell if I feel hot or cold.

"Why did you open it if it was my letter?" I ask. I look for my brother to be somewhere, anywhere in the room, but it is only my mother and me.

"That's hardly the point, Sadie."

I go quiet at this, think for a minute. "No," I say, surprising myself. "It *is* the point. Or part of the point. You need to leave some things to me."

"The point is that you deliberately lied to me. That you deliberately did something I told you not to do and that–"

"It doesn't have anything to do with you!" And now my voice is rising, and my mother is getting that clamped expression on her face that I can't handle. "It doesn't, Mom. It's about me. I want to learn to drive. I don't want to wait until I'm eighteen. And then have you come up with some other excuse."

We look at each other, the only sound, the hitch of my breathing.

"So you took this course anyway." She takes her hand away from the laundry pile. Quiet infuses her voice. "Who signed the permission slip?"

"I did."

She nods, brushes past me. I can almost hear what she's about to say, so I rush in.

"I know you're deeply disappointed in me, Mom. But guess what? You can't keep me twelve forever."

"I don't want to–"

I hesitate, teeter, fall. "Ollie didn't die because he was driving a car."

At first, I think my words have no effect, but then her face crumples. I step back, feeling the outlines of my dresser behind me.

"I know that," and her voice sounds torn open and wet. "I *know* that," she seems to be saying to herself.

"Mom," I begin, not sure where to go.

"Do you know what I would give to bring him back?"

"Probably what I would give," I whisper, but I don't think she hears me.

"I thought . . . I shouldn't talk about it . . . about him . . . with you. I told your father that we had to . . . I thought we should try to let you live the most normal life you could."

"I *want* to talk about Ollie," I say to her, and now my own voice is trembling. "I thought . . . when you wouldn't talk about him . . . I had this idea that you blamed me."

My mother lifts her head sharply at this. "How could you ever think that? I never said that, did I?"

I shake my head. "No."

"Then why would you ever think something so preposterous, why would you–"

"Because *I* blame me."

"*Why?*" she whispers.

"Because I didn't want to go swimming with him. Because I didn't want to draw the ocean. Because . . . it's stupid, I know that."

"Oh, God," my mother says. She is looking at me in a way I think I've seen only once before, the look she gave me when she found me lying under the Hanging Tree with my leg broken. Suddenly, I think how it's been forever since I have drawn my mother, and how much I would like to draw her face now, with all her lines and angles and planes, and then draw myself and see how different we look. I think I would see something like the same guilt in both our faces.

She moves forward then and wraps her arms around me until I don't know which one of us is holding the other.

Chapter Twenty-Five

"Sadie," Travis calls out, and I stop my progression down the hallway.

"Later," Lila murmurs, nods at Travis, who is approaching. He comes to a stop, smiles his sweet, slow smile that I like to think is only for me. He tilts my chin up. I lower my eyelids. When our mouths are a breath apart, I can't help myself.

"Did you have anything to do with trashing Ryan's car?" I ask.

His thumb under my chin slips away. "What?"

"Ryan. Fryin' Ryan," I say. I am jostled from behind, and I stumble into Travis, who puts a steadying hand on my shoulder.

"I called your house, like, three times last night. Where were you?"

"Just tell me, Travis."

"Sadie. It was a *joke*. The kid's a freak." He puts his fingers over my mouth. "And no, I didn't actually do it. Miller and Henrick and a couple of other guys did it in their free period. Okay?" He lowers into the voice he uses on our late-night phone conversations.

"Okay." I lean into him again, let him wrap his arms around me.

"Awwww. They're so cute," I hear a girl giggle. I smile, turn my head into Travis's shoulder, inhale the sweet smell of laundry detergent.

"Here's Freakshow now," I hear him murmur, and even though his voice is quiet, the words feel like they are hammering straight into my head.

I pull away, watch Ryan coming down the hallway. He looks neither right nor left, his eyes fixed at a slant somewhere above everyone's head, his briefcase swinging lightly by his side. Today, his T-shirt is bright green, with the words WOULD I LIE TO YOU, BABY? scrawled in bloodred across his chest.

"Jesus," Travis says, looking at Ryan. I drop my eyes to the smudged no-color floor and take a tiny step backward.

❧

The bell rings, and all around me, students clatter their brushes into jars of watered-down turpentine, strip off their smocks. I concentrate on my still life, on the eggplants and pumpkins, on the way their shapes interlock. I focus on their colors, how the orange is not really a true orange, and how the purple really holds a note of black. I keep on painting.

"Remember, your portfolios are due next week," Mrs. Byrd calls over the rising din. Her voice spirals upward. "Portfolios," she entreats again as everyone files out. I jam the knuckles of my free hand into my lower back against a fluttering twang of cramped muscles. The animation drips from Mrs. Byrd's face as she bends laboriously, picks up a scrap of paper from the floor. Straightening up, she catches my eye.

"Don't you need to get to class, honey?" she asks now.

I shake my head. "Lunch. Can I stay?"

"Of course." She moves over to my easel, her pale green caftan fluttering as she walks. "Very nice, dear. Don't forget to ground the eggplant with some shading. But very nice." Then she scoops up a forgotten brush on the rim of the easel next to mine. The bristles have already stiffened into spikes, and my teacher exclaims softly, carries it promptly to the sink. "I'll be in and out, dear, if you want help," she calls as she leaves.

I chew my lip a little, study my eggplant.

There is a slight shuffling noise to my right as my brother unfolds himself from the windowsill.

"Don't look at me like that, Ollie," I mutter.

❧

I hover in the doorway to the Student Center, squeeze my elbows closer to my body as people push past me. I search for Ryan, my eyes zooming left and right.

"Maybe he's not here today," I murmur, ignoring a girl with wispy brown hair who frowns at me.

"He's right in front of you," Ollie says softly. I don't need to look where he is pointing. My eyes must have skipped and wandered across the blur of Ryan's features, as if the pieces of his face did not add up to a whole.

I stand for what feels like forever, and Ollie stands with me, motionless for once. The I take the most direct route. Which involves walking by my table.

"Hey, Sadie," I hear Erica call, but I do not turn. If I do, I know I will stop, will let myself be hooked and reeled inward, so I press on. I am dimly aware that Travis is rising, holding out a chair for me, and I am touched, painfully so.

I approach Ryan's table, pause, wait.

He looks up. Silence enshrouds us both.

"I'm not just your friend on the beach," I blurt out. I imagined this scene over and over last night. I imagined Ryan delighted, Ryan angry, Ryan mocking me. But he says nothing, just pushes his glasses higher up on the bridge of his nose, regards me like I am a not very interesting bug under a microscope.

"So, can I sit here?" I ask, after I can't stand this anymore.

"This isn't your table, mermaid," he reminds me, almost

patiently, as if I have misplaced the knowledge temporarily. "Don't sacrifice yourself needlessly."

"What are you even talking about?"

He jerks his chin at a point behind me, but I refuse to turn. "They're waiting for you. Your jock boyfriend might even come over here and carry you off."

I try to ignore that. "Maybe I want to sit here."

Silence again.

"You know, Ryan," I say, finally, my voice rising. "You're a real pain in the ass sometimes. I want to sit here. I want to talk to you."

"About?"

"About anything. Maybe I want your opinion on what's going on in the Middle East. Maybe I want to know what you think about this new idea that we share some chromosomes with dogs. Maybe I want to talk to you about the imagery in T. S. Eliot's *The Waste Land.* Have you *read* that one?"

I kick free a chair and thump myself down into it. I don't look at him as I fumble through my backpack and grab the brown paper bag that holds my lunch. I swing it onto the table with a satisfying smack, feeling something give inside the bag.

Ryan is polishing his glasses with the edge of his green T-shirt. Slowly, he puts them back on his face, touches the rims with both forefingers, as if trying to see straighter. He looks at me. "Yes, I've read *The Waste Land.*" His voice is soft, open, and the light in his face is almost too much to bear.

I nod, lean down to zip my bag closed, and manage to risk a glance at my table. Erica is leaning over Travis, her mouth moving furiously. Christie is staring openly, while Ruth can only give me quick, nervous glances, as if she is afraid I am contagious from all the way across the room.

I tear off a tiny strip of my lunch bag, begin twisting the

brown paper between my fingers. "I read your poem last night," I say quietly, without looking at him. I had read it over and over that night after I had said good night to both my parents, after they had both hugged me extra hard and long, my mother's eyes still red-rimmed. Now I say, "I liked it. I really liked it. Especially the part when the sky turns 'techno-color gray.'"

"What did you like about that?" His voice is hesitant, and I wonder if he's ever shown his poetry to anyone else.

"I don't know. I just . . . liked the way it sounded. It had a good sound to it." I look at him earnestly. He is listening to me with a concentration that I've seen him use on books, so I add, "I think in colors sometimes, so I could see what you meant."

He nods after a minute, stirs his plastic spoon through the cup of corn on his lunch tray. "Thanks."

"You're welcome." I tear off another strip of my lunch bag, just as two guys and a girl walk by the table. I think I recognize them from Miller's party, and I try not to react as they stare at me and Ryan. I am much too aware of the vast reaches of the whole Student Center, of the hundreds of hostile faces, aware in a way that I haven't been since my first week here. "So," I say, and work at keeping my voice normal. "Did you get in a lot of trouble with your dad?" I desperately want a Coke, but the soda machine is at the far end of the cafeteria, and I can't fathom how to walk that distance and back. Instead, I reach around to pull out the half-empty bottle of water that I bought after gym class.

And that's when I see Lila come through the double glass doors. She walks over to our table, begins to shed herself of books and bags, no lunch, as usual. She checks her watch just as Erica extends her arm in my direction. Lila twists, finds me, stands still. Vaguely, I am aware that Ryan is answering my question, but his words bleed into each other like colors washed out by rain.

I don't wave or nod or make any motion. I don't want to see if she will respond or not. Instead I straighten up, unscrew the water-bottle cap with fingers that suddenly feel numb. I drink the rest of the bottle in clumsy gulps.

"Sadie," Ryan is saying, and I get the feeling he has said my name more than once.

I set the bottle back on the table, look at him blankly. "What?"

"The rescue team's coming. They've sent in the big guns. You're like Persephone, you realize. You've spent long enough in hell." The words are pure Ryan, flippant enough, but there is a tremor to his voice.

"Who's coming?" I murmur.

"Lila."

I slowly turn my head, pinpoint her walking in a precise, delicate way. Her hands are loose and empty at her sides. It seems like an hour passes before she arrives.

"Sadie," she says, stops two feet away from my chair. She swings her long hair over her shoulder, and the faint smell of her lavender shampoo, like the scent of spring in this colorless cafeteria, drifts on the air.

I lift my eyes, meet hers, and watch her deciding on what to say. I didn't realize how I had liked her calling me *Caldwell.* I didn't realize how she made this place feel so safe, how much I am going to miss that feeling. Then I look back over at Ryan. His mouth is working downward, and I realize he is trying to reassemble his face into its usual mocking expression. I give him time to collect himself, shrug a little at Lila.

"Sadie," she says again. And her voice is like a summons. "I need to talk to you about our English presentation."

Relief is unwinding into me. I can legitimately tell Ryan that I have to meet with Lila about our English presentation, and get up and leave, and then I will only have sat here for a few brief moments, not long enough to have done any damage. I can explain to Travis that I felt sorry for Ryan. I can ignore whatever Erica will say. I can go back to being normal.

"So sit down," I say, and there is a challenge in my voice that I didn't know would be there. I knock a chair free with my hand, push it toward her.

Lila locks one ankle behind the other, stands perfectly poised on one foot, like some Sphinx. Her face is set in that impassive, stone-statue manner, her gray eyes wide and assessing. I think about the first time I saw her and how little I knew her then.

Suddenly, she grins at me, swings herself into the chair, looks directly at Fryin' Ryan.

"What's up, Ryan?"

He stares at her in complete shock, as if a sunflower just nodded its head at him and spoke. I give him a swift, short kick under the table.

"Hey, Lila," he manages.

I breathe again. If I were painting right now, I think the air would be the exact shade and hue of freshwater pearls. There is a crinkling sound as Lila plunges into my lunch bag.

"Carrot cake?" she asks, holding aloft a dark, crumbly square, squishy with frosting.

"Your guess is as good as mine," I reply.

Chapter Twenty-Six

This is the first day in four years that I don't draw the ocean.

Snow is falling when I climb over the seawall, and I can't help but think how Ollie would have loved it. We never saw snow in California. Except on postcards. The Atlantic is churning out little white huffs of waves, and I have the beach all to myself.

I close my eyes and try my hardest to call up Ollie, but just as in life, my brother proves to be elusive, slippery, fleeting. I think of the first time we saw snow, when we were seven and we got to accompany our father on one of his business trips, that time to Montreal. We flew straight into a frozen world of winter and spent most of our days huddled against each other, our thin California skin swaddled in layers and layers of wool.

"Ollie, Ollie, Ollie, all home free," I whisper now, hoping that he will appear.

No use.

I sink down to the cold, solid-packed sand, close my eyes, and think of that day, the last words that I spoke to my brother, as I turned away from him, so sure he would always be there.

"I'm sorry, Ollie," I whisper now. "For not going swimming with you. For not helping you with Lycee. For not even looking at you the last time you spoke to me." I fumble at the barriers of jacket and scarf and sweater until I reach my skin. I unhook Lycee's dog tag from around my neck, hold the cold metal between my fingers. "If I could take that day back, I would, Ollie. Before you ran out the gate, I would have called you back. I would have promised to go swimming with you. By the time I had changed, that stupid car would have come and gone already, and we could have gotten Lycee back. I would do anything, Ollie, if I could just have that day to start over."

My voice shreds apart, and I open my eyes. My brother is sitting next to me, tracing patterns in the sand.

I look at him for the longest time, at the dark gold of his skin, forever the color of summer, while the warmth of my own is fading. At the seven freckles scattered across his left arm that I used to play connect-the-dots with while he was sleeping. At his eyes, still a pure green, while my own have slipped into more of a hazel color. I think of how I know no one's face better.

"Ollie," I whisper again. "I'm so, so sorry that I let myself lose you."

The snow comes softly, gently, a hazy screen between us. Big, dreamy flakes cling and pile in the folds of my jacket as I walk to the edge of the water. I stand for a long time, watching the snow fall like light across the water.

I raise my right hand and throw Lycee's dog tag as hard as I can. The oval flips over and over through the air, the silver metal glinting briefly before it vanishes under the waves.

When I turn, Ollie is gone. Ryan is climbing over the wall, heading toward me. Instead of his trench coat, he is wearing an orange jacket, ridiculously bright in all the whirling whiteness. I can't understand how I could have even once mistaken him for my brother. Ryan waves vigorously.

I smile, hold up both my hands, fingers stretched toward the sky.